Engaging Mr. Darcy

AN AUSTEN INSPIRED ROMANTIC COMEDY

Austen Book 1

Rachel John

ACKNOWLEDGMENTS

My husband loves Pride and Prejudice as much as I do. His advice and suggestions have been amazing and I'm super lucky to have him. I'd also like to thank my critique partners, Franky A. Brown, Krista Noorman, Crissy Sharp, and Amy Klaus for their input on this one. Also a big thanks to my beta readers, Victoria Frantz, Robin Cranney, Rachael Eliker, and Michelle Higham. The author community is an awesome place to be.

CHAPTER 1 ♥ GOOD LOOKS AND BAD TEMPERS

The insistent dinging was followed by an exasperated voice. "Hey, can I get some service around here?"

Elsie Bennet sighed. She'd left the front counter for thirty seconds to check on an order, so how long had the guy possibly been waiting?

"Be right there," she called, speed walking back to the counter, careful to jump over the hole in the rubber anti-slip floor mat.

When it came to impatient pizza guests, they were usually on the plump, frazzled side. She stopped in her tracks and had to rein in her urge to stare. Despite the unpleasant grimace, this guy was gorgeous. His crossed arms only accentuated his muscles.

"I was starting to think this place was abandoned."

Elsie pasted on a smile. "Well, I'm here now. How can I help you?"

"I called ahead. Do you have my pizzas ready?"

"You're Darcy?"

His jaw tightened. "It's my last name."

She hadn't meant to sound incredulous, but clearly, she'd hit a nerve. "Um, I'll go check." It was a placating gesture. She knew Gerald had barely put them in the oven. A glance at the timer told her she'd have to stall the angry hot guy for another ten minutes.

She returned to the counter and took a fortifying breath. "I'm sorry. They'll be coming out of the oven in a few minutes." *Or so.*

"You promised the pizzas would be ready at six forty-five. We're five minutes past that."

"Again, I apologize. We have some premade salads you might be interested in. I could add one to your order. No charge."

He leaned against the counter. "I don't want your wilted salads. What about a discount on the pizzas?"

She glanced down at his expensive watch and back up at his perfectly styled hair. "Do you need a discount?" It slipped out before she could stop herself.

He stared her down. "I'd like to speak to your manager."

"There's no manager here. Just me and Gerald." With occasional appearances by a stingy owner who didn't like to give out discounts. Even offering the salad was pushing her luck, wilted or not.

"Of course there's no manager here. I should have guessed."

Elsie stood a little taller. "You should be nice to people who prepare your food."

"Are you threatening to do something to my food?"

"No. I'm not the one making your food. I don't even box it up. I can guarantee your pizzas won't come out defiled. By me." She grinned, watching him squirm a little. Honestly, the food was so bad here, eating it was punishment enough. Which was why the place was dead on a Saturday night.

"Well, I don't need your guarantees. I need the ten pizzas I ordered." He kneaded his forehead, as if this was the most stressful thing he'd ever encountered.

Wow, this guy needed yoga, or a nap, or something. Yes, it was annoying that Gerald took forever, but he was the owner's son and she'd learned the hard way that complaining about him did nothing.

"Just a few more minutes, sir."

"You said that already."

There were no other customers at the counter, so Elsie turned to find something, anything else to do. The drink cups were low. A miracle. She went in the back to open a new box and pulled them out of the plastic sleeve.

Elsie reluctantly returned to the counter with them, trying not to watch the guy pace.

She could hear Gerald humming in the back. He even sounded slow. *Seriously, Gerald?* She put the cups down and went to see if she could prod him along. Like maybe with a red-hot poker.

"Psst. Gerald!"

Gerald stopped staring at the wall and turned to grin at her. "Hi, Elsie."

"Yeah. Hi. Any chance those pizzas could come out a few minutes early? The guy's kinda in a hurry."

Gerald pointed to the timer. "Five minutes left."

She glanced back and noticed the customer was now leaning over the counter, craning his neck to see what was going on in the back. "Hey!" he called. "Can you at least ring me up so I can take them when they're ready?"

Elsie jogged back to the front and ran the impatient guy's credit card. Fitzwilliam Darcy. That must've been a fun name in elementary school. Did he go by Fitz? Or did they call him 'I throw fits'? The smirk died on her face when she looked up and saw him glaring.

***

Will Darcy lingered in the kitchen, breaking down pizza boxes and wiping the crumbs from the granite counters. Anything to keep from having to go out and mingle with Charlie's friends. Charlie's goofy, free-spirited personality attracted people like moths to a porch light. This party was only one example. How he managed to get this many guests to come to his housewarming party was insane. Who would want to drive to this little town in the middle of nowhere for one night? The ugliest corner of California, too far from the beach, or L.A., or culture. Meryton, California: famous for nothing, especially not its pizza. He'd eaten half a slice and thrown the rest in the garbage.

Unwillingly, his thoughts flitted back to the dark-eyed girl with the bad customer service skills. He shouldn't have been so impatient with her, no matter what urgent texts he was getting from Caroline and Charlie. Nobody was starving to death when he got back. Considering how little he wanted to be at this party, he should have taken even longer, maybe stayed to chat with the pretty Pizza Palace employee. Say that ten times fast. Okay, now he was really losing it.

"Fitzwilliam Darcy, are you hiding out in this kitchen?" Caroline Bingley sauntered in and leaned against the counter. "I

5

can't believe you left me to the wolves out there."

"Wolves," he scoffed. "More like chattering monkeys."

"Well, either way, Charlie is looking for you. He wants you to meet his new friend, Dr. Lucas. The good doctor lives down the street and stopped by when he saw all the cars outside." She couldn't hide her amusement. "Charlie invited him in."

"Of course he did."

"Come on, Will." She grabbed his arm and dragged him towards the kitchen door. "Technically this is your housewarming party, too."

She had a point. Not wanting to hang out with Charlie in some pay-by-the-week motel dump, Will had found him a house where the owners were desperate enough to let them rent month-to-month. He often did that for his migrating friend. After all, what was the use of having connections in real estate if he didn't use them?

It was immediately ten degrees hotter and three times as loud in the living room. "Charlie's over here." Caroline led the way and he followed, avoiding eye contact with several women who eyed him curiously.

His friend's curly blonde mop appeared around the corner, where he was animatedly speaking with an older gentleman wearing a hideous celery-colored polo under a dark cashmere vest. Everything about the guy screamed bad taste and pretension. Not that pretension was always a bad thing. Will was pretentious. But he liked to think his was understated.

"Will, come over here." Charlie smiled as wide as Texas and slapped Will on the back. "I've been telling Dr. Lucas all about you. Dr. Lucas, this is Will Darcy, my oldest friend."

"Nice to meet you." Will shook the doctor's hand, trying not to let his eyes wander around the room in search of escape routes.

"Charlie tells me you're in real estate?"

Will nodded, shoving his hands in his pockets. The doctor's eyebrows stayed animatedly high, apparently waiting for Will to elaborate, something he was not eager to do. Anyone willing to live here couldn't appreciate real estate. "Are you a medical doctor?" Will finally asked.

"Oh, no. I have a Ph.D." Dr. Lucas said.

"In what?"

"Medieval literature. A fascinating subject. Take, for example, the concept of chivalry. From my studies I found that the ideal knight would uphold honor, courtesy, and piety above all else—"

"Dr. Lucas, Charlie, if you'll excuse me." Will retreated back through the crowd and headed for the patio, letting out a deep breath. He'd ask for Charlie's forgiveness later. There was a couple on the far side of the patio, but they ignored him and he did likewise. Taking a chair on the other end, he took out his phone and sent his sister, Gianna, a text message.

Everything ok?

Yep. How is Charlie settling in?

He loves it here. Of course, he loves it anywhere. I'm sure he'll shed a few tears when he finishes up his work and moves on.

And you'll follow him, grumbling the whole way.

Will smiled. She knew him too well.

Get some sleep.

I will. Just as soon as I'm done clubbing. A girl's gotta have her social life.

How she could still joke about that after everything that had happened, he'd never know. But it seemed to help her cope.

Talk to you tomorrow, party animal.

He turned at the sound of someone nervously clearing his throat, and the medieval literature guy was standing there with a goofy smile on his face. Great, now he'd have to apologize for not staying for the lecture on chivalry. How ironic.

"Will, I already mentioned it to Charlie, but since you're staying with him, I wanted to extend an invitation to you personally as well. I'm the block watch captain for the neighborhood and we're having our annual block party this Friday night at the park at six. There will be food and dancing. We have lots of single ladies on this street, including my daughter, Charlotte. I'm sure she'd be excited to meet you."

Will wanted to decline right then, but since the guy had brought his single daughter into it, he figured a less offensive strategy would be to hedge.

"That's nice of you. I'll talk to Charlie about it." *And by that, I mean, I'll make sure to be busy on Friday night.*

"Excellent. Have a good night, then!"

Elsie headed straight to the shower, more than ready to get the pungent smell of grease and pizza dough out of her hair. Her mind kept rewinding her conversation with the irate pizza customer. It was like God realized he'd given the guy too much natural good looks and decided to skimp on the personality.

Elsie was more than happy to be only passably pretty. *At least I'm a decent person.*

Hunger finally had her reluctantly turning off the hot water and she quickly dressed and toweled off her hair before padding into the kitchen.

Her sister, Jane, turned and smiled. "How was work?"

Elsie wrinkled her nose. "As terrible as it usually is. Speaking of, I have the perfect idea for a new T-shirt." Elsie ran to her desk and started to sketch, an evil grin spreading across her face. All thoughts of food were forgotten for the moment. She felt her shoulders relax as she drew a perfect set of eyebrows arched down in insane displeasure. Wavy hair, just the right length, dimpled chin. Muscular arms bearing down on a counter, fingers splayed. But what to call him?

Jane followed her into the room. "Two more custom orders came in and one of them paid the rush fee. If you have the time, we really need it done tonight. Pretty please?"

Elsie let out a large sigh and set aside her revenge piece. She'd get back to it later. "What do they want done?"

Jane set down the email printout and backed up slowly, fingering her long blonde braid.

"Is it that bad?" Elsie asked before looking down at the multiple paragraphs of instructions. "They want five teenage girls recreated as puppies?"

"They sent photos," Jane called. "I'll make you dinner."

Elsie sketched out the general idea of what she wanted, and then turned on her computer screen and began to research dog breeds. Who in their right mind wanted to recreate their daughter and her friends on a T-shirt as puppies? But that's how she and Jane had garnered a loyal following. Making things no one else could.

One of the girls had glasses with fun frames. An easy detail to transfer. They would each need something identifiable. Something to stand out and represent their look…

She barely noticed when Jane set down a burrito plate next to her. What time was it? With a yawn, she took a bite and glanced at the bottom right corner of her screen. 11:30. Someday, her late night eating habits were going to catch up to her. But she couldn't bring herself to eat another slice of pizza or another plate of the restaurant's tasteless spaghetti. They were lucky to be the only pizza joint on the east side of town.

Jane popped her head in again. "I'm heading to bed. Why don't you finish it in the morning? I'll even take your shift checking in on Mom and Dad."

It took all her willpower to shake her head at Jane. "No, Janie-girl. I promised Mom. You help out enough as it is."

Jane turned to go, but stopped at the end of the desk and picked up Elsie's drawing. "Who's this?"

Elsie fought the urge to grab it and leaned back in her chair. "Some mean customer I had tonight at the restaurant."

"Someone new in Meryton? Is he as handsome as he looks here?"

Elsie shrugged. "He was a jerk. I just, I liked his face. That's all."

CHAPTER 2 ♥ DEBT AND OTHER UNPLEASANT THINGS

Mrs. Bennet beamed when Elsie walked through the door. "I'm so glad you're here. I think the toilet upstairs is clogged. Would you be a dear and check it for me?"

Elsie forced a cheerful expression and headed upstairs. Yes, it bothered her to be treated like a maid, but she preferred it over Jane's role, which was to sit and listen to their mother gossip and complain for hours on end.

They were lucky to get off with a daily morning visit, considering they only lived three houses down from their parents and her mom needed constant attention. Her dad was the one living with chronic pain, but he wasn't the one mooning around the house, wringing his hands.

Elsie glanced out the bathroom window, looking down on the backyard where her dad was standing there with his walker, adding water to his bird fountain with a hose. Weather permitting, that's always where he could be found, finding an excuse to do something outside. Every year on his birthday, Elsie gifted him with another reason to hide out there. The barometer last year. The hummingbird feeder the year before.

The toilet seemed okay, but the counter was a mess, covered in toothpaste marks and bottles of hair product. This was Lydia and Kat's bathroom. They should be taking care of it. But they were rarely home these days. Just long enough to make a mess before heading off on Lydia's quest to chase stardom.

Elsie took the stairs two at a time and jumped for a final landing on the tile below.

"Elsie, don't clunk down the stairs like that. It's very unbecoming to men."

Elsie grinned at her mom. "I'll make sure to remember that next time there's a single guy over here."

"You should. Lydia brings them home in spades. Last week she had a poker tournament here and the whole house was filled. She won fifty dollars. It's those acting skills, I tell you."

A thousand different cutting remarks filtered through Elsie's head, but she decided not to say any of them. Maybe she'd treat herself to ice cream later. "Where is Lydia?"

"Another audition. She and Kat took a road trip to L.A. They'll be back tomorrow."

"Where are they staying tonight?"

"Oh, I don't know. With friends, I suppose. She has my credit card if they need a hotel. I told her to pick a nice one. No sense in staying somewhere cheap."

A headache started as she walked to the window to escape her mother's smug and oblivious smile. There was no money for things like that. There was no money for live-in help, which might become a necessity in the coming years. Even with her dad's disability insurance, the monthly payments only covered the basics, and the policy ran out at age sixty-five. Ten years seemed like a long time to prepare for that, but was it really?

Once again she felt guilty for pursuing her T-shirt business with Jane instead of doing something practical and financially secure with her graphic design degree. She was twenty-six. Maybe it was time to stop dreaming and get a steady job.

Elsie walked out and grabbed the vacuum from the hall closet and headed straight for the office. She vacuumed with one hand while signing into her parent's bank account with the other. Their passwords were laughably simple. Elsie had thought about suggesting they change them, but it was easier to keep up the pretense that she didn't meddle.

Their balance was even lower than last month. Five-hundred dollars left and they hadn't paid the credit card yet. She opened another screen and signed into their credit card account. "Forty-five hundred dollars!"

Good thing the vacuum drowned out her swearing. Restaurants, pedicures, boutique clothing stores. They all had one thing in common: Lydia. And now she had Kat taking up the same habits. At least practical Mary had a full ride scholarship to UCLA.

Elsie shut down the computer and dragged the vacuum out of the room, hitting the door frame on her way out. Her mother glanced up, looking irritated when she stomped into the room and dropped the appliance with a clunk, letting the handle fall to the floor.

"What is it, Elsie?"

"You can't let Lydia use your credit card anymore. She needs an allowance. Or better yet, she should get a job and stop mooching off you altogether. She's eighteen now. She should open up her own credit card and max it out."

Mrs. Bennet sniffed. "Lydia is so talented. One of these days she's going to make it big and then she'll be the one paying for us. I don't mind helping her out a bit now."

Elsie put her face in her hands. She couldn't tell her mother what she really thought, that Lydia was not talented, and didn't have the work ethic or connections to make up for that fact. "It's not a good idea. You guys don't have the money to let her keep doing this."

"Talk to your father about it. It's his decision."

Elsie's shoulders dropped. She didn't like to stress him out with things like this, but it would have to be done. Her mother might be hoping she'd give up, but Elsie's stubborn streak was stronger than her mother's diversionary tricks.

She turned and headed straight to the backyard. "Dad?"

He was done with the fountain, and she found him under the citrus trees with his fruit picker, a tool she'd bought him last Christmas. On good days, he could hold up the long handle and pick an orange or two.

"Would you mind getting the higher fruit?" he asked.

She took the tool and angled it up into the branches, picking oranges and mulling over the best way to broach the unpleasant subject. Better to get it over with.

"Dad, Lydia shouldn't have access to your credit card. She's spending more than you and Mom have."

He harrumphed in a non-answering way. "Talk to your mother about it."

"I did. She said to talk to you."

He waved an arm. "The balance is only five-thousand dollars. What harm can she do?"

"Five-thousand dollars' worth. It's almost maxed out. How will you pay for it?"

"A little bit each month. Isn't that how it's usually done?"

Elsie shook the branches a little harder than she meant to and several oranges fell, one of them hitting him on the shoulder. "Sorry."

"No harm done. But why are you worrying about this, Elsie? Lydia's not independent like you. She'll probably be at home for a few more years until she catches some rich guy smitten enough to marry her. Then she'll be his problem."

"And you'll have no savings. You're supposed to be saving."

"The house is paid off. Maybe we'll do a reverse mortgage."

"At least make her get a job. Otherwise, she'll talk Mom into opening up another credit card. She's not going to just stop spending."

Mr. Bennet turned the orange back and forth in his hands. "She has a job. She's an unpaid actress."

"That's not funny, Dad." But Elsie smiled in spite of herself. Lydia had been an extra on several movies, and once, the back of her head was on screen for ten seconds. For all her time and trouble? A catered lunch.

"Elsie! Elsie, are you out here?" Mrs. Bennet came around the corner waving an invitation in the air. "Oh, there you two are. Gather up some of those oranges. We have a new neighbor and you need to take some to them."

"I'm sure they have their own oranges, Mom."

Mrs. Bennet's face clouded. "I'm sure they don't. These are better than anything they'd find in the store. And aren't you even curious about who lives there?"

Mr. Bennet sighed. "Well, obviously you want to tell us, so be out with it, dear."

"Oh, who asked you?" Mrs. Bennet shook a hand at her husband and turned back to Elsie.

"There are two single guys renting a house down the street. Dr. Lucas says they're very handsome and rich."

Elsie tried to suppress a laugh and ducked her chin. "Mom, if two guys are renting a house together in California, it sounds like they're already taken."

"What does that mean? Oh…no, no. Dr. Lucas would have said something. He was hoping to introduce them to Charlotte at the block party on Friday. I want you and Jane to beat him to it."

"No way."

"Elsie!"

Elsie was about to stalk back into the house to avoid an argument, but then she thought about how much her mother hated that she and Jane were still single.

"All right, Mom. I'll do it. But first, I'm helping you pay off the credit card this month, and when Lydia gets back from her trip, we're closing the account. No more giving Lydia your credit card."

Mrs. Bennet's mouth gaped open and closed and then she huffed. "Fine."

"No, Elsie. I won't let you pay that amount," Mr. Bennet protested.

Elsie turned on him. "Don't worry. It won't happen again. The next time Lydia hits you up for money, tell her to come talk to me."

***

Charlie had accepted Will's insistence that they not go to the block party. They'd even made other plans. But then two girls apparently showed up with oranges, and suddenly Charlie wanted to go. Typical. Charlie got excited over the simplest things.

"Go ahead. But I am *not* going to that stupid block party tonight."

"Come on, Will. Be my wingman. I have to see Jane again and just showing up on her doorstep would be weird."

"Like how she showed up on your doorstep?"

"That was different. She was welcoming me to the neighborhood."

"Then why didn't you get her number?"

Charlie frowned. "I forgot. I was so caught up in the moment, I forgot to ask. Plus, her sister was with her. It would've been tacky."

Will went back to looking at real estate listings on his laptop. "Then go to the party. You don't need me. You've never needed me to meet women."

"Her sister's pretty cute, too."

"Pass."

Charlie let out a sigh, but he let it go and walked off. It was for his own good. Will refused to feel bad. Besides, if Charlie liked this girl, he could walk down to her house. Will settled deeper into the couch and pulled up his calculator app, comparing interest rates against hypothetical home loans. It took him a minute to realize Charlie had come back in to stare at him, a mischievous look on his face.

"What now?"

Charlie sat down on the coffee table, tapping his phone on his knee. "I didn't want to have to do this, but I just texted Caroline and told her I was going to the block party, and that you'd be sitting on the couch all alone, watching movies tonight. She said she'll be done grocery shopping in a half-hour and can't wait to join you."

Will snapped his laptop shut. "I can't believe you would use your sister's crush on me for your own evil designs."

Charlie laughed. "But it's so convenient."

"When is she going to stop babying you and go home, anyway? You can buy your own groceries, you know."

"She's leaving tomorrow morning. Which means tonight is her last chance to spend time with you. Do you want it in a public place or in a snuggly place? It's an awfully comfortable couch you're sitting on."

"I hate you."

Charlie only laughed harder.

"I will not be sitting on this couch all night anyway. I found a hiking trail right behind the house and I was planning on going for a run."

"What about after that? Come on, Will. Come to the block party. They're hiring a D.J."

"Stop it, you're making it sound worse."

***

"Look who I found in L.A.!" Lydia sang out, sailing through the door Friday afternoon. She had on a new pair of sunglasses, her hair was freshly highlighted, and she had shopping bags swinging on each arm. "Mary's home for the weekend."

"Let me help you with those." Elsie reached out and took the shopping bags, and Lydia smiled benevolently, not aware that Elsie had no intention of giving them back.

Kat and Mary came in the door, and Elsie gave them each an armless hug before walking out, still holding the designer bags. "Wait a minute." Lydia shoved past them and followed Elsie outside. "Where are you going with those? I need them in my room upstairs." As if Elsie was her personal assistant.

Elsie turned around in mock surprise. "As soon as you pay me for them, I'll be happy to return them to you. Jane and I might try on some things first, though."

Lydia did what she did best. She scrunched up her face and screamed at the top of her lungs. "Mom! Maaahaam!"

Normally, Elsie didn't mind the spectacle. The other neighbors were used to it, but she nervously glanced at the rental house, hoping the two new guys were gone for the day.

Mrs. Bennet wasn't hurrying as fast as Lydia had hoped, so she turned and charged Elsie. Lydia wasn't a fast runner, but she also wasn't burdened down with shoe boxes and Gucci bags. Elsie sprinted as quickly as she could to her front door and ran inside, slamming it shut in Lydia's face.

"You won't get away with this, Elsie!" Lydia yelled through the door. "Like you even care about fashion."

"I care about money," Elsie called back. "I had to pay off Mom and Dad's credit card and then close their account. So hand over that useless card, get a job, and start paying me back."

"You're the worst!" Lydia screamed and banged on the door, muttering something about how no one understood her.

Elsie wouldn't put it past Lydia to try to break in. She hid the bags in an upstairs closet behind the Christmas decorations, and then reached for her buzzing phone, pulling it out of her back pocket.

"Hi, Mom."

"I never agreed to you treating Lydia this way. You need to apologize to her right now and return her things."

Elsie took a calming breath. "I would never steal from her. I promise I will hold onto everything and give it all back as soon as she pays me for them. I already explained it to her."

She heard her mother relating her words back to Lydia in a soothing tone while Lydia blubbered. "But they might be out of season by then!" Lydia wailed into the phone. "It's none of her business. She doesn't live here anymore, and she shouldn't be bossing you around, Mom."

No, that's now your job, Lydia. "Don't worry. I won't be interfering again. But Mom, I'm holding you to our agreement. Jane and I went over and met the new neighbor and we're going to the lame block party tonight. So no more credit cards. Lydia's old enough to get one of her own."

She hung up as Lydia pierced her eardrum with another long wail.

CHAPTER 3 ♥ CLEAN UP

Dr. Lucas spotted Will and Charlie the instant they approached the park. "So glad you could make it!" he called out.

Charlie gave him a gripping handshake and a pat on the back. "We're happy to be here, Dr. Lucas. I believe you wanted us to meet your charming daughter?"

Will turned and eyed Charlie, but Charlie only shrugged, murmuring, "Might as well get it over with."

Dr. Lucas successfully pulled his daughter out of the crowd and brought her over. The poor girl looked mortified, and Will instantly felt less annoyed with her.

"This is my Charlotte. She cuts hair at the barber shop in town."

"It's a salon, Dad," Charlotte corrected him. She held out perfectly manicured fingers and shook Will's hand, and then Charlie's.

"You should be dancing," Dr. Lucas nudged. He looked meaningfully between his daughter and Will. The makeshift dance floor on the basketball court was only a few feet away.

"I'll dance with you," Charlie quickly offered. He took Charlotte's hand and lifted it up in the air, weaving her through a group of people embarrassing themselves to a Justin Bieber song.

Will let out a sigh of relief. He wouldn't have left Charlotte out in the wind, but he also loathed both Justin Bieber and dancing in public.

"Well, Will. There are lots of other girls I could introduce you to. The Bennet girls are right over there. They have, can you believe it, five single daughters."

Will knew the man was trying to be helpful, but his knowledge of all the young single women in the neighborhood was a bit creepy.

"Thanks, Dr. Lucas. I think I'll be fine. Is that the snack table over there?"

Dr. Lucas didn't hear him. "Elsie! Elsie Bennet!" He tried to wave over a dark-haired girl who smiled back and instantly retreated, pretending she misunderstood his hand motions. She looked familiar, but Will only saw her face for a second before she lost herself in the crowd. Lucky girl.

It was time Will did the same. "I'll see you around, sir." Will took off and weaved through the crowd until he found a partially empty park bench. He put his back to the two kids stuffing their faces with cotton candy on the other end of the bench and did some people watching.

Charlie was still out on the dance floor, this time with a beautiful blonde woman closer to his age. Will wondered if it was the esteemed Jane, the neighbor who'd brought the citrus. As usual, Charlie looked like he was having the most fun of anyone anywhere, and he probably was.

If Caroline Bingley wasn't waiting for him back at the house, poised to spring on him, Will would leave right now. He sighed. It seemed like everywhere he went, he was perpetually unsatisfied. Did other people feel this way?

***

Elsie stood next to Charlotte and took a sip of her Pepsi. "Can I go home yet?"

Charlotte laughed. "Not until I get to, and I'm pretty sure I have to stay after and clean up."

Elsie twirled her finger in the air. "Yay, us!"

"Jane looks like she's having fun."

"Yeah, she couldn't stop talking about Charlie last night. They are disgustingly adorable together."

"What does he do?" Charlotte asked.

"He works for an earthquake warning company. They're putting sensors in Meryton. Government contract. I'm not sure how long that takes, but I doubt he'll stick around when the job's done. I wouldn't."

"Poor Jane. She wouldn't be brave enough to follow him, even if he asked."

They watched Charlie whirl her around and then pull her close, whispering in her ear. "I don't know," Elsie said, tilting her head. "I've never seen her like this. But I'd sure miss her. None of my other sisters are exactly roommate material."

As if to prove her point, Lydia ran by, knocking into Elsie's elbow. Soda spilled down Elsie's front.

"Now I really am leaving."

"Ah, man." Charlotte sighed. "I don't want to stand here by myself."

"I'll be back," Elsie promised. "I haven't seen my mom yet, and I have to prove I came." She dropped the soda can in a nearby garbage and threaded her way through a group of teenage girls with a terrible case of the giggles. She followed their gaze to a glaring guy, sitting alone on a park bench. The rude customer from Tuesday night? Was it actually him? He turned to look at her and confirmed it. She'd recognize that scowl anywhere.

"Ask him to dance," one of the girls whispered.

"No way," her friend whispered back, giggling. "He's, like, super old."

"And super yummy."

"But he's so grumpy."

"I'll cheer him up," another one said with a grin.

"Give it up, girls," Elsie said, not bothering to lower her voice. "He's as grumpy as he looks. And super old, like you said."

'I-Throw-Fits' lifted his chin and leaned back on the bench. "Look who's talking. Are these your coworkers from The Pizza Palace? They look about the right age to work there."

"Oooh!" The girls laughed and glanced at Elsie, waiting for her to zing him back. Nothing at the party was remotely as exciting as this.

"What's your name again? Fitzgerald? Fritz? How did your pizza party turn out?"

He stood up and walked over, using his full height to look down on her. "The pizza was bland. You have a little something on your shirt."

Elsie glanced down at the wet spot in the middle of her grey T-shirt and groaned. Seeing Mr. No-Personality had made her completely forget about the soda.

He smirked and walked past her. "Nice to see you again."

***

Will watched her go through the front door of a little gray house across from the park. She was completely not his type. A small town girl with a dead-end job, too mouthy for her own good. And yet there was something about her that got his blood pumping. Maybe it was just the adrenaline of a good verbal spar, but he liked the spark in her eyes when she stared back at him, matching his glare. And he liked her dark hair, pulled back in a loose braid hanging over one shoulder. Like a warrior princess.

She came out of the house a few minutes later wearing a different shirt, and he tried not to stare as she jogged back to the party, throwing a few skips in before rushing up to Dr. Lucas's daughter, Charlotte. They linked arms and chatted to each other. He realized she was the one Dr. Lucas had attempted to wave over to him earlier. A Bennet girl. It took him a minute to dredge up the name. Elsie. Elsie Bennet.

What would she do if he arranged an ambush with Dr. Lucas? It might be another hour before he could drag Charlie out of here. Might as well have a little fun.

He spotted Dr. Lucas and went over to ask for an introduction to Elsie Bennet. Dr. Lucas's face lit up and he immediately led Will over to where Elsie and Charlotte were standing.

Elsie's eyes widened at the sight of him, and she whispered something to Charlotte before putting on a polite face for Dr. Lucas.

"Elsie, dear. This nice young man asked to be introduced. Will Darcy, this is Elsie Bennet, a good friend of my Charlotte."

"Nice to meet you." She stared up at him, the tone of her voice conveying how much she didn't mean the words.

"Would you like to dance?" Will pressed.

"Not really."

Charlotte sucked in a breath, and Dr. Lucas frowned.

"What she means is that—"

Elsie cut Dr. Lucas off. "What I mean is that I don't want to dance. With you." A ghost of a smile crossed her face, and then she excused herself and walked away.

Dr. Lucas apologized over and over, but Will waved him off. "It's okay. Trust me, I'm fine. Charlotte? Do you want to dance?" Charlotte glanced from Will to her friend's retreating back. She shrugged. "Okay."

He took her hand and led her onto the dance floor, glad a slow song was playing for once. Charlotte placed her hand on his shoulder and looked up at him with appraising eyes. "She's not normally that rude. Why does she dislike you so much?"

"Maybe she's only nice to her friends. I've found her to be incredibly rude the few times we've run into each other."

"If you've run into her before, why did you ask my dad to introduce you?"

Will smiled. "I'll plead the fifth on that one."

Charlotte narrowed her eyes at him but didn't question him further.

He looked over and saw Elsie standing next to a man sitting in a wheelchair, her hand in his. He immediately thought of his sister, Gianna.

Charlotte saw him watching them. "That's her dad. He has rheumatoid arthritis and can't stay on his feet too long without it hurting."

"Oh."

They didn't speak again until the end of the song. Charlotte raised an eyebrow. "Take care, neighbor."

"Same to you."

A hand slapped down on his shoulder, and he turned to see Charlie's grinning face. "Hey, Jane and I were going to head back to my place to watch a movie. Have you met anyone you might want to…" he dropped his voice, "bring along?"

Will looked over at Charlotte, but she was well out of hearing range and wasn't looking in his direction anymore.

"Nope."

"Don't worry. Caroline will be thrilled to be your date."

Will gave him a shove and followed him over to meet the famous Jane Bennet. The one who'd been glued to his side for most of the night. She was as fair as Elsie was dark, but their eyes and noses were the same shape.

"Did your sister want to come?" Charlie asked, quickly glancing back at Will.

Jane shook her head. "She's staying to help clean up."

"Oh." Charlie winced. "I feel bad leaving her to do that."

"Me too." Jane glanced at an overflowing garbage can. "She told me to go on ahead, but…"

Will rolled his eyes. A goody-two-shoes match made in heaven. If they were staying, he wasn't heading back on his own to fend off Caroline's advances. After the housewarming party, she'd *accidentally* knocked against him in the hall, hanging onto his shoulders to keep from falling. He was pretty sure the knowing smile and the hands slowly running down his biceps had nothing to do with maintaining her balance.

"Why don't we go home and relax until the party's over and then come back to help clean up?" Will suggested.

"Great idea. Now I remember why I keep you around, Will."

"More like I keep *you* around."

"Save the bromancing for later, guys." Jane grinned at them and patted Charlie on the chest. "Although you two are adorable."

Will laughed. Maybe Jane Bennet wasn't just a pretty face. He hoped she'd take it well when Charlie up and left one day. Charlie didn't mean to be a heartbreaker, but unfortunately, his enthusiasm for life and tendency to live in the moment meant he could be just as happy somewhere else, with someone else.

Will was much more careful about relationships. Which was why he rarely dated.

***

Elsie shuddered at the sticky mess clinging to her gloves and hefted another garbage bag into the dumpster. It didn't quite make it over the side and fell back to the ground, spilling open. She let a few choice words slip and bent down to clean it up. Charlotte owed her big time.

"Let me help you with that."

Elsie whirled around and skidded on a food wrapper, losing her balance and falling on her bum. She looked up at the one person she wished would drop dead. "You."

"That's quite the potty mouth you have there."

"I was talking to the garbage, so it felt appropriate."

Will Darcy reached down and lifted her back to her feet. One gross gloved hand gripping another. What was he doing here? He obviously hated the party. Why stick around afterward to help clean up?

She went back to picking up garbage and flinched when they reached for the same soda can. "It's fine. I got this."

He shook his head. "I don't mind."

"No really. You should go... somewhere else."

He laughed. And then he ignored her advice and went back to picking up garbage.

"Isn't this kind of thing beneath you?" She should shut up now, but her mouth wasn't listening. "I mean, I take out the trash all the time at The Pizza Palace. But you ... I'm sure you have a janitorial staff to do that kind of thing for you."

"Where do you think I work?" he asked.

"Somewhere where you don't have to deal with a lot of people, but you still make a lot of money." She almost slapped a hand over her mouth at that one, but she remembered the gloves just in time.

"Intelligent observation."

"I'm right?"

He shrugged. "I'm an investor. Mostly in real estate. But I do have to talk to people from time to time."

She put a hand on her hip and instantly regretted it. These clothes were going straight into the washing machine. "Then what are you doing here? Interested in Meryton real estate?"

He scoffed, clearly finding the idea laughable. "No. I won't be buying anything here. But Charlie is like family to me. And he often has to go live in new places for months at a time. I tag along for the fun of it."

"I didn't think you knew what fun was." Dang it. Could she ever shut up?

He shook his head at her. "I'm thinking customer service is a bad choice for you. Isn't there something else you can do?"

"As a matter of fact, Jane and I own a business. But it's new. And I still have to pay my bills." *And bail my baby sister out of trouble from time to time.*

"What kind of business?"

She held out her shirt, showing him the cottonwood tree on the front. Each leaf was a different color. Like a tree made of Skittles.

He stared back, puzzled. "What am I looking at?"

She jabbed at the front of her shirt. "We design T-shirts."

"Oh."

His silence was speaking volumes. He thought her business was dumb. Little did he know she'd sold two hundred of this design in the past two months. And every month they were selling more and more. But she didn't have to justify her life's work to him. She tossed the last soda can in the dumpster and walked off.

CHAPTER 4 ♥ PAY UP, MONEY BAGS

It was late, but after a shower, Elsie's fingers itched to finish up the sketch of Will and turn it into a T-shirt. Knowing Will, he'd sue her if she tried to make a profit off the image, but that didn't mean she couldn't make a T-shirt for herself and wear it around. She studied her drawing, absurdly proud of how she captured both his attractiveness and his bad temper. After uploading the drawing to Photoshop, she perfected the digital version, adding color and polish. She found the perfect font for 'The Me Monster' and cackled in delight. Feeling guilty for wasting so much time on a revenge project, she ended up pressing and packaging up ten shirts to take to the post office in the morning. It was two a.m. before she finally shut down the computer and turned off the light to the office, just as the front door clicked open and shut.

Jane was sneaking in and Elsie crept up behind her, following her down the hall.

"Late night?" she asked.

Jane screamed and whirled on her sister. "Don't do that! And what are you still doing up?"

"I was going to ask you the same thing."

Jane blushed. "We went for a walk, that's all."

"Quite a long walk."

"It wasn't a big deal. Will tagged along. He was afraid to go back to the house by himself."

"What? Is he afraid of the dark or something?"

Jane laughed. "No. It has something to do with Charlie's sister.

She's been at his new rental house for a week, helping him set up."

"And Will's scared of her?" Elsie couldn't imagine Will being scared of anything. Annoyed, yes. But not scared.

Jane shrugged. "I can't see why. I met her. There's nothing scary about her. She's this petite little thing, and very friendly. We talked for a half-hour while the guys watched football. She said she was headed to bed when we came back to clean up the party."

"Weird." Not that any of it mattered. All she'd meant to do was ask about Jane and Charlie and somehow it came back to Will. Ah, of course it had. Jane was no fool. Elsie followed Jane to her bedroom and leaned against the door frame. "A two-hour walk, huh."

"Yep."

"Just walking?"

Jane rolled her eyes. "Stop it, Elsie."

"So how much of that two hours was spent making out on our porch?"

Jane sputtered out a denial, but the deep blush on her face told the real story.

Elsie laughed and said goodnight.

***

There was a light rap on Will's door and he froze in the middle of taking off his jeans. He should have been quieter.

He zipped them back up and went to his door. "What is it, Caroline? I was asleep."

"Room service," a high falsetto called out. "Open up."

"Charlie!" Will unlocked the door and whacked his friend on the arm. "It's about time."

Charlie had the sense to look sheepish, and Will crossed his arms. "You need to be careful with Jane. You're leaving in a couple months."

"You worry too much."

"And you worry too little."

A door opened down the hall, and Caroline poked her head out, squinting her eyes against the light coming from Will's room. "Did you two just get in?"

Charlie nodded. "You should have come with us. We had a great time."

27

"*You* had a great time because you had a date," Caroline said, throwing Will a quick look. "Besides, cleaning up after a bunch of stupid Meryton teenagers is not my idea of fun."

"Agreed." Will's mind immediately flitted back to watching Elsie fall on her backside in front of the dumpster, and he smiled. Well, it wasn't all miserable.

Caroline left her room and sidled up to Will in her silky boxer shorts. Will wasn't immune to her beauty. Caroline was an attractive little thing, there was no denying it. But she also held more than a slight resemblance to her older brother and was the most determined woman he'd ever met. At least when it came to him. He was fairly positive she thought she could wear him down if she tried hard enough.

"You need a shower, Will." She leaned into his chest and sniffed his shirt, her hands coming up to grip each side.

"Well, I'm off to bed." Charlie gave Will a wink and headed down the hall. The jerk.

Will unleashed himself from Caroline and retreated behind his door, practically closing it on her face. "Goodnight," he called out, turning the lock. He should really consider finding new friends. Preferably ones whose sister didn't stare at him like the last brownie on the dessert tray.

***

Elsie rang up another order and slid five pizza boxes across the counter. Just a few more hours. A few more hours and she could wash the pizza smell out of her hair. It was a shame about those three cavities earlier this year. Who knew simple dental work could be so expensive without insurance? Also expensive: Shopaholic sisters. The only recent major expense she didn't regret was the beautiful new heat press that would take their business to the next level.

There were so many online T-shirt businesses. It made her proud that she and Jane had held on, carving out a spot in the vast internet shopping universe and cultivating loyal repeat customers. Someday soon, she'd be able to quit here and work on the business full time. Until then, she'd continue to prod Gerald along and deal with the irritated customers waiting on their pizza.

The bell above the restaurant jangled and a set of familiar

giggles met Elsie's ears. Lydia and Kat. They were followed by two good-looking guys in leather jackets.

"Hi, Elsie!" Lydia called out. "I want you to meet our new friends."

"Can you hook us up with some free pizza?" Kat asked, without shame.

"Kat, is that any way to treat your sister?" One of the guys pulled out his wallet and stepped up to the counter. "I'm Jeff Wickham. It's nice to finally meet you. Your sisters talk about you all the time."

"Only good things," Lydia added, with a laugh. She and Kat exchanged glances. Elsie had no doubt that was a lie.

"This is Denny," Kat said, snaking an arm around him. "We met them in L.A. last week and they came down to visit us. Isn't that so amazing?"

"Amazing," Elsie echoed, turning to give Gerald the order for two pepperoni pizzas.

She turned back around and tried not to stare at Jeff, who was leaning on the counter, watching her with appreciative eyes. She was too old to let her heart jump at a little male attention. The guy was friendly, that was all.

"Lydia says you have a T-shirt business."

"Yep."

"She's probably wearing one now," Lydia said, fiddling with the free pizza-shaped magnets on the back of the soda fountain. "Under that hideous work apron."

Elsie blushed. Wearing the Will revenge shirt only seemed like a good idea in the comfort of her home. All her earlier bravado slipped away, leaving only embarrassment.

They stared at her expectantly and she felt dumb with her arms wrapped protectively around her waist. She was being paranoid. Lydia and Kat hadn't even met Will, and even if they had, it wasn't a perfect likeness. She slipped off her apron and squared her shoulders, letting them have a look.

"The Me Monster?" Kat asked. "I don't get it."

"Me either." Lydia went back to playing with the magnets. "Elsie has a strange sense of humor, Jeff. You'll have to get used to it."

"I get it," Jeff said, meeting Elsie's eyes with a knowing smile. "Looks just like him. How do you know Will Darcy?"

Elsie's eyes widened. "Promise you won't tell him." She put the apron back on quickly. This was the worst kind of coincidence.

Jeff leaned over and lightly tapped her on the nose. "As long as I get a shirt like that."

"Oh, I don't know. I only made this one for me. I wasn't planning on selling them."

"You should. It would serve him right. He's a twit."

The bell jangled again and Jeff, Denny, and her sisters stepped back so she could help the new customers. She tried to focus on her job and not the nagging worries over what she might have let loose. How well did Jeff know Will? And what had Will done to make Jeff dislike him so much? Did he go around offending people everywhere he went? Well, that one was an easy guess.

Gerald finished with her sisters' pizza order just as the bell jangled again.

"Are you guys wanting these to go, or are you eating here?"

"Here," Kat said, just as Lydia said, "To go."

Jeff laughed at them, sliding an arm around each of their shoulders, but then his face froze as he caught sight of the group lingering by the door. "I think we'll take them to go."

Elsie looked at the door and smiled at Jane and Charlie, The Sunshine Twins, as she'd decided to call them. Will Darcy stood next to them, locked in a death stare with Jeff. She was used to seeing Will peeved, but this was peeved times infinity.

She handed the pizzas over to Jeff, noticing how his whole body screamed stress and discomfort. "What's wrong?" she whispered, touching his wrist.

He put on a forced smile. "It's nothing. But I do want that T-shirt. I'll trade you for a story about Will. The truth shouldn't be hidden behind an apron. You see right to the heart of people. That's a special gift."

He gave Denny a knowing look, and the two of them attempted to steer Lydia and Kat around the group at the door. Lydia, oblivious as always, would have no part of it.

"Jane! Aren't you going to introduce me to your man? The two of you are adorable together."

Lydia stuck out a hand, the bracelets on her wrist jingling a musical rhythm. "I'm Lydia, Jane's baby sister."

"Charlie Bingley. So pleased to meet you." Charlie turned her wilted offering into a firm, friendly handshake and was as equally pleased to meet Kat. "You have so many sisters," Charlie said with a laugh.

Jane nodded. "You haven't met Mary yet, but that's all of us. All five."

"And all beautiful," Kat added, with a giggle.

"Oh, I don't know," Lydia put in, ever so tactfully. "Mary's kind of plain, especially now that she'd turned all emo on us. Jane's always been known as the beauty, but I'm definitely the curviest." With that, she gave a little shimmy and laughed overly loud.

Charlie beamed, but Will stared at the ceiling and ran a hand through his hair, obviously impatient to get the chitchat over with. Elsie shared his discomfort, but she also didn't like seeing him judge her family.

Jane put out a hand to Lydia. "Aren't you going to introduce us to your friends?"

"Oh, yes." She turned, looking around for Denny and Jeff, who had suddenly become interested in a faded poster on the wall, it's plastic covering smeared by little pizza fingers.

"Jeff. Denny. Come back over here!"

They obliged, hands in pockets, never taking their eyes off Will's face.

"This is Denny Hanes and Jeff Wickham."

Charlie's smile faded a little and he looked at Will, finally catching onto the mood in the room. "Jeff Wickham?"

"You should leave," Will said. "Now. We don't need to be introduced."

"Well, who are you, the Queen of Sheba?" Lydia said, immediately puffing up. "We'll leave when we're good and ready."

Jeff pulled on her arm. "Let's go eat our pizza, baby girl. Don't worry about him. I never do." He and Denny successfully steered the girls out of the restaurant.

***

Will could feel the blood rushing in his ears. He had so many things he'd planned to say to Jeff Wickham if he ever saw him again. Things he'd planned to do to him, like break his kneecaps. But the moment had come and all he did was stand there like a frozen corpse. It wasn't fair. It wasn't fair garbage like Jeff got to go on with a normal life, while his sister had to—

31

"Will. It's okay." Charlie patted him on the back. "Let's get some pizza."

"I hate the pizza here." He looked up when he said it, catching Elsie's glare. She'd been touching that piece of trash, whispering with him. Who knew what kind of things Jeff might have said about him? Will could warn her, but she'd probably think he was lying and immediately run into Jeff's arms. Jeff was good with women. Good at reeling them in and getting them to believe anything he said.

"How are you, Elsie?" Charlie drummed out a rhythm on the faded red counter top. Will could tell he was eager to put the tension behind them.

"Doing fine. What are the three of you doing here?" Her eyes flitted to Will for half a second before she turned her attention back to Charlie.

"Jane wanted to come see you, and I was hungry, so it was an easy decision." Charlie grinned broadly and leaned on the counter. "What's good here?"

She glanced over at Will again. "Nothing's good here. I would especially not recommend the Chicken Parmesan. It's been sitting awhile."

Jane started laughing and couldn't stop. "This is why I love you, Elsie. You always tell it like it is."

Will was about done with the whole Bennet family for the night. He knew his irritation was firmly rooted in Jeff Wickham showing up, but Elsie was right in front of him, and he needed to let off steam. "Are you saying we should go somewhere else to eat?"

Elsie turned and glared. "I don't know. You're pretty free with telling other people to leave. It shouldn't be hard to figure out your own plans."

He glared right back. "You don't know what you're talking about."

"Hey, now, Will. She was making a joke. Take it easy." Charlie motioned up at the board. "How about a large Hawaiian pizza. Will can pick off the pineapple."

"Whatever." Will crossed his arms and turned his back to the counter, hating being the third wheel, hating the smell of this horrible excuse for a restaurant, and hating the uselessness he felt at knowing he'd let that piece of crap, Jeff, walk out.

The police had promised they'd take the case seriously. They said Jeff would get real jail time. But none of their promises meant anything now. Jeff had served his thirty days. A slap on the wrist if there ever was one.

"When do you get off, Elsie?" Charlie asked. "You should come hang out with us after work."

Jane nodded vigorously.

Will didn't turn around to see Elsie's reaction. He already knew what it would be. But Charlie and Jane still wanted to make her the fourth to their happy party. It was so humiliating. For both of them.

Will needed to leave here. Charlie didn't need his company. He could go home and help Gianna. Only she didn't need him either. She'd found a new happiness, in spite of everything. The only one who couldn't find happiness glared at him in the mirror every morning.

Charlie and Jane wandered over to an arcade game against the wall, and Will turned to watch Elsie in the back with Gerald. Whatever she was saying, she was using slow, simple words and big hand gestures. He didn't know who he felt sorrier for, the girl stuck working with a slow cook or the slow cook constantly treated like a child.

She came back to the counter and sighed. "Make yourself comfortable. It might be a while. He usually puts the pineapple pieces on one by one, like he's doing a puzzle."

"It's all right. We can wait."

His calm response seemed to make her suspicious, and that made him laugh. "I'm sorry I was impatient the other night. Charlie was having a housewarming party and all the hors d'oeuvres were gone in the first five minutes. I volunteered to go get more food."

She nodded in response and fiddled with a stack of paper menus. It would take more than a half-hearted apology to thaw the hard feelings she'd developed toward him. Why did he want to thaw them? That was a mystery better left unsolved.

"How's your T-shirt business going?"

She glanced up and shrugged. "It's fine." She'd been so proud of it the other night, but now there was only hesitation and insecurity in her face.

"Did you draw the tree on that shirt you were wearing last night?"

33

She nodded. "Yeah, it's the tree in my front yard, only, a little more colorful. I posted about it on our website, and now we get requests for other people's trees. A lot of people want shirts with their bonsai tree on the front. I know that probably sounds dumb to you."

"No. If there's a market for something, you follow it. That's business."

The phone rang, and she walked away to take an order over the phone, occasionally sneaking glances back at him. He watched her wind the long strings from her apron around her fingers. When she turned to the side and leaned against the wall, her apron moved, revealing her grey T-shirt underneath. Assuming it was another one of her creations, he studied it and his breath caught. No way, it couldn't be what he thought it was.

He waited until she hung up and walked back.

"So, what big plans do the three of you have tonight?" she asked, a mean sparkle in her eye. Considering all the ribbing he'd given her, it was a well-deserved jab.

"Go ahead. Tease me because your sister stole my best friend. Would it be better if I ran around frantically looking for a date to even out the numbers?"

"Isn't that why you're here?" she asked with a grin.

He ignored the question. It wasn't meant to be flirtatious, only mean. "So, can I see today's T-shirt?"

Pretending to misunderstand him, she took out her phone and pulled up her website. "We do have a T-shirt of the day, actually. Here, take a look."

Smart girl. But she didn't know he'd already seen most of what she had on under that dirty apron, and he wanted her to admit it. He leaned over and looked at her screen, taking advantage of the close proximity. While she was distracted, he pulled aside the apron a few inches, and she immediately backed up and hugged herself. "What do you think you're doing?"

"Calm down, princess. I just want to see the T-shirt you have on now."

"That's not how you ask! Are you a three-year-old? You ask with words, not with your hands. I swear, it's like I'm babysitting again."

He smirked. "I did ask. You deliberately misunderstood me."

"Well, now that I understand you, the answer is no."

"Why won't you show me the shirt?"

"Because I don't like you and I don't want to."

They stared at each other, and he swallowed, taking in her flushed cheeks and rigid stance. If he gave up now she'd likely go home and burn the thing. There were no other customers in the shop, and Charlie and Jane were busy going head-to-head in Pac-Man. It was now or never. And yet, what could he do? Not like he was about to jump the counter and chase after her, as fun as that might be.

"I'll give you a hundred dollars."

She rolled her eyes. "You're being ridiculous."

"Two hundred."

She sized him up and then leaned forward, holding out her hand, palm up. "Fine, money bags. Pay up."

He withdrew his wallet from his back pocket and pulled out two crisp bills, laying them on her palm. She kept her face neutral as she folded them up and shoved them into the front pocket of her jeans.

"Okay, here's the big reveal." She was trying to be sarcastic, but she wasn't as good at hiding her nervousness as she thought. Looking down, she untied the apron and pulled it off.

Oh, wow. She'd completely captured his likeness. And dubbed him 'The Me Monster.' When he finally pulled his eyes away from the shirt and met her stare, the mutual embarrassment was palpable. "It's just this one," she murmured. "I won't be making more of them."

He nodded and looked away, ready to call it a night. Charlie and Jane were finished with their game, and Elsie quickly retied her apron before heading back to check on the pizza. He sat down in a booth and wondered who he was angrier with, the girl who saw the worst in him or the guy who matched her description.

CHAPTER 5 ♥ SOB STORY

Elsie couldn't wait to melt into bed, but she got a text from Lydia as she was drying her hair with a towel.

Jeff and Denny wanted me to invite you over. We're making cookies.

Did she want to go spend quality time with Lydia? Not really. But it did intrigue her that Jeff wanted to see more of her. Outside of this week, new people were a rare occurrence in Meryton, especially single guys. She only wavered for a few seconds.

I'll be there in ten. Thanks.

She reapplied her makeup and combed out her hair, pulling it into a loose bun. What to wear? Something comfortable, but flattering. She left a note for Jane, not wanting to deal with the immediate questions a text message would invoke.

She could hear Lydia cackling from behind the front door of their family home as she walked up. The door was locked so she rang the bell. Kat answered, her mouth full of chocolate chip cookie.

Denny popped up behind Kat and tapped her on the shoulder. He ducked when she turned to look and then she chased him out of the room, the two of them laughing and squawking. Maybe coming wasn't the best idea. She was already forming excuses to leave after a few minutes.

"Elsie! So glad you could make it." Jeff patted the spot on the couch next to him. He was like a calm oasis, separate from the giggle fest going on all around him. She sat down next to him and leaned back into the couch cushions.

"You changed your shirt."

Elsie looked down. "Well, I try to avoid smelling like pizza for longer than necessary."

He leaned over and sniffed. "I don't mind pizza, but I have to admit, you smell great."

She laughed and pushed him back. "I don't know you well enough for you to be sniffing me."

"Fair enough." He reached for a cookie off the plate on the coffee table and offered her one. "How was the rest of your shift?" His eyebrow raised, and she knew he was subtly referring to Will Darcy's presence at the restaurant.

"Will saw the shirt."

"No." Jeff slapped his knee. "I can't believe you showed it to him. That's awesome."

"I wish I'd never worn the thing at all. He must have gotten a peek at it when I turned to the side or something. I refused to show him at first, which was super humiliating, but then he started offering me money."

"How much?"

"Two hundred dollars."

Jeff's jaw dropped. "No way."

She pulled the bills out of her purse, and he doubled over laughing. "That's my girl. Taking his money and insulting him at the same time. You're my new best friend."

She laughed too, but a twinge of remorse nagged at her. She didn't regret anything she'd said to Will's face. But talking about him behind his back, laughing at him? That wasn't usually her style.

Jeff must have seen her hesitation. He reached out and touched her arm. "Will uses money to get what he wants. You shouldn't feel bad."

"Tell me about Will. How do you know him?"

Jeff hesitated. "You'll sell me one of those shirts?"

"I can't. I promised him it was the only one."

Jeff rolled his eyes. "Let me tell you my sad story first, and then you can decide if you want to keep that promise to him."

She doubted she'd change her mind, but her curiosity was enough to hear him out. "All right."

"Will and I were actually good friends as kids. We grew up on a nice street in Brentwood. He lived in a million dollar house with a pool in back and a tennis court, and I lived down the street in an apartment we could only afford because it was rent controlled, and my grandparents started living there in the fifties.

"Anyway, at some point he realized I was super poor. He accused me of only coming over so I could use his stuff. I was ten. I didn't know how to respond to that."

"Of course not," Elsie murmured.

"He went to a private school, and I went to public school so it wasn't hard for him to avoid me. But, he has a younger sister, Gianna, and we stayed friends. Will didn't like that."

Elsie folded her arms. "But there's gotta be more to it than that. The look of pure…"

"Hatred? Yeah, Will hates me. I think it's easier for him to blame me for what happened than to look at his own role in it. One night, a few years ago, I'm out with Gianna and she gets a call from Will. He realizes I'm with her and starts yelling, telling her to come home. She's flustered and hands me the phone. Like I want to talk to him. I try handing it back and don't see the car turn in front of us. I remember braking hard, then nothing. Next thing I know, I'm waking up in the hospital. And while I was unconscious, Will was busy throwing his opinions and his influence around. I got charged with reckless driving and reckless endangerment and spent thirty days in jail."

Elsie covered her mouth with her hand. "That's horrible."

Jeff nodded. "You know what hurts the most? Gianna went along with it. That was the end of our friendship. She finally chose him over me. Blood's thicker than water, I guess."

Neither of them said anything after that, both lost in thought. Lydia, Kat, and Denny came and squeezed in next to them, ready to start a movie, and Mrs. Bennet came out to lecture them about all the noise. It was hard to take her seriously with the gigantic hair rollers mounted on her head, but they promised to quiet down.

Elsie fell asleep halfway through the movie and woke up with her head against Jeff's shoulder. She looked up and gave him an apologetic smile, but he only grinned back, his eyes shining into hers. She'd only known him for a few hours, but their connection had been instantaneous. Jeff was the kind of person who made you feel like you'd known him all your life. Will was missing out.

***

"You're leaving?"

Charlie walked in and sat on the bed, messing up Will's carefully folded stacks of clothes.

Will pulled a shirt out from under him and gave him a dirty look. "Work calls. My flight is at ten."

It wasn't just about work, but Charlie didn't need to know that. Yes, Will needed to check on renovations at one of the apartment buildings he'd purchased last month, but more importantly, he needed to get out of Meryton. He couldn't be somewhere Jeff Wickham was currently squatting, and he needed space from Elsie. With Charlie and Jane together, Will was bound to run into her again and do something stupid, like demanding to see what she was wearing. A small smile escaped. Man, he was dumb. Like every other red-blooded man, his impulse control went into toddler-mode over a woman, and he wouldn't let that happen again.

"How are you getting to the airport? I'd drive you, but I have to be on the jobsite in twenty minutes. Why didn't you tell me sooner?"

"It's fine. I called a cab."

Charlie leaned against the chipped dresser. Needing a place fully furnished meant every piece in the house had seen better days. "Well, come back as soon as you can. It will give me an excuse to throw a party."

Will raised an eyebrow. "If that's supposed to lure me back, you may want to come up with a better strategy."

Charlie grinned. "You'll be back. Who else would keep me in line?"

"That's right. The dark cloud that occasionally blots out the incessant sunshine you carry around."

"You and your metaphors," Charlie said. "I'm going to grab something to eat while I still have time. And seriously, don't be a stranger."

Whatever. Charlie couldn't get rid of him even if he tried. Besides Gianna, Charlie was the closest thing to family in his life. He'd trade all the money he'd inherited for one more day with his mom, for one more chance to connect with his dad.

A honk from outside let him know the cab had arrived. Early. That never happened. He shut his suitcase, not worrying about double checking the room. After all, he'd be back. Charlie threw him a granola bar as he passed the kitchen, and he ran out the door and handed his suitcase to the cab driver to put in the trunk. He glanced at Elsie and Jane's house one last time before forcing himself to forget about her and her aggravating T-shirt.

***

Mr. Bennet sat at the table with his laptop, an amused expression on his face. "Come here, Elsie. I have to share this with somebody or I'll burst."

"What's so funny?"

"You remember Collin, the kid who stayed with us one summer?"

"Your cousin's stepson? Of course, I remember. He followed Jane around the whole time, repeating everything she said until she'd scream."

"Well, hopefully he's matured, because he's coming to visit us next week. I guess he won the lottery, and his financial advisor suggested he lay low for a while. His friends and family are constantly hitting him up for money."

"How much did he win?"

"Five-hundred million."

A glass crashed to the tile floor in the other room and Mrs. Bennet came in, fluttering her hands. "Five-hundred million? I sure hope he likes Jane as much as he used to. Can you imagine how well off we'd be if she married into that?"

"Now Hilda, that's exactly the kind of thing he's coming here to avoid."

She ignored Mr. Bennet and ran out of the room. "I have to call Jane. Elsie! Will you clean up this mess before someone steps in the glass?"

Elsie went to get the broom and dustpan, thinking back on memories with her step-cousin. Little worm. He used to lick the salt off his fingers and reach back into the chip bowl. When he realized it bothered her, he'd stare at her while he did it, a grin on his face. It figured someone like him would win the lottery.

She headed home after cleaning up the glass and found Jane on the couch, surrounded by mailing boxes.

"Did Mom call you with her big news?"

Jane looked up. "Yes, she sure did. It's all set. We're having a fall wedding with a huge open bar reception. Vera Wang is going to design my gown."

"I wonder what ol' Collin looks like now," Elsie said, picking her way through the box maze.

"Come see. I Googled him." Jane turned her laptop screen around and Elsie sat down, pulling it onto her lap.

"Wow. He's lost all his hair. But maybe that's a good thing. He had so many cowlicks, his hair never knew what to do with itself."

Jane cocked her head. "Don't be so judgmental."

"I'm not judging, I'm noticing. Five-hundred million dollars. I can't even imagine that."

"Three-hundred million. He took it in a lump sum after taxes."

Elsie laughed. "Wow, you really have been studying up on him. Charlie's not good enough now that Collin's coming to town?"

Jane blushed. "You have to stop teasing me about Charlie. We've only known each other a few days."

"Janie-girl, as few dating opportunities as we get around here, we have to celebrate when we can."

Jane's eyes lit up. "Speaking of, since when do you and Lydia hang out? You told me that's where you went last night, but I have to know. Are you interested in one of her guy friends?"

Elsie wanted to deny it, but she wanted someone to talk to more. "Maybe. Jeff Wickham seems to get me. And that's hard to do."

Jane bit her lip. "I asked Charlie, but he wouldn't tell me what the deal is with Will and Jeff. Just that Jeff wronged Will's family. He seems to think Jeff should be in jail." Her cornflower blue eyes held concern.

Elsie's laugh came out bitter. "Wronged him? More like Will's controlling and mean." She was happy to have the whole story so she could clear Jeff's name. Charlie would side with Will no matter what, but Jane needed to know the truth.

CHAPTER 6 ♥ NOBODY IS NOBODY

The crew lead, Tim, walked Will around his new investment property, showing him the retiled pool, the newly striped parking lot, and the updated landscaping. Even with as much money as he was dumping into it, someday it would all be worth it. The surrounding neighborhoods were a lot nicer than this old place, and as soon as they re-named it and started renting out apartments again, it would pay out for years to come.

"How many tenants have to be grandfathered in at the old rent price?" Will asked.

"Forty-five."

"That many?"

"Would've been more. Fifteen tenants so far wanted into the renovated apartments after they saw them, even with the higher rent. Mostly single professionals too busy to move to something nicer. This gave them that chance. And it gives us fifteen more apartments to gut."

"How are we doing on the budget for each renovated apartment?" Will asked.

Tim shrugged. "We were doing fine until I realized we'd have to special order the toilets. They have to be compact to fit in the space. You'd think smaller toilets would be cheaper, but they're not. I wanted you to look over some flooring alternatives, see if we can find something less expensive to make up the difference."

Will frowned. If they were going to skimp on anything, he didn't want it to be flooring. But he'd trust Tim to give him the details first.

He followed him up to an apartment on the second floor and got lost in the minutiae of a project this size. It wasn't until he'd returned to his quiet and impersonal hotel room that gloomier thoughts took hold. He pulled out his phone and texted Gianna, needing a little bit of her warmth and good cheer.

How R U?

She texted back quickly, as she always did. *Excellent as always. What's the matter?*

Who says something's the matter?

This gal. Now spill.

Am I an egomaniac?

Probably. But the fact that it worries you, says you're not.

Thank you, I guess.

You're welcome. But seriously. Should I call you? My fingers are already tired.

Sure.

Ten seconds later, his phone rang and he sighed. "Hi, Sis."

"So, what's this egomania stuff about? Charlie calls you stuck up all the time and it's never bothered you before."

"It wasn't Charlie. It's nobody. Just some girl in a pizza shop."

"If it's bothering you, I doubt she's nobody. And nobody is nobody, Will. Don't talk about people like that."

"How'd you get so smart?"

"Good genes." She laughed. "So, tell me about this girl."

"What girl?"

"Very funny. I love how we play these games, like you still think I can't read you."

He rubbed his head and reached over for his bottled water. "Her sister is dating Charlie. So, in a couple months, when he cheerfully breaks up with her and moves on, both girls will hate me anyway. It's not even worth talking about."

"Ahh."

So much was dangerous about that sound when it came to Gianna. "What is it?"

"So she's not just some girl in a pizza shop. Charlie might move on, but that's not your style. This girl scares you."

"Caroline Bingley scares me."

"Yes, but not like this. What's her name?"

"Nope."

"Come on. This might even tempt me to come out and pay Charlie a visit."

Now that was big. Travel held all sorts of pitfalls for Gianna, things the average person never had to consider. The fact that she brought it up was huge.

"I would love to have you come visit. But I'm not there. I'm in Phoenix, checking on a couple properties, and after that, I'm coming home to see you."

"So you're running."

"Gianna." She wasn't going to let this drop. She wanted him to find someone, and unfortunately, she understood better than anyone how alone he often felt. "I barely know this girl. And she despises me." He didn't mention Jeff Wickham showing up. That was something he'd spare her.

"She just hasn't gotten to know the real you, yet. You don't let anyone see that. You won't even let me tell people about all your charity work."

"Gianna."

"I know, I know. Your secret's safe with me."

"Okay, I'm hanging up now. We can discuss this in gruesome detail tomorrow night over dinner."

"I'm holding you to that. Goodnight, Will."

***

Elsie stood in front of the washing machine, gripping 'The Me Monster' shirt and debating whether to throw it in the wash with her other clothes or toss it behind her into the trash. The image was still saved on her computer, an even scarier thought.

She heard Jane come in the front door and chucked the shirt in the load before slamming the washer door shut. So she'd wash it and hide it in the bottom of her drawer. It would end up being a funny story for later. It didn't matter that Will's face upon seeing it had sort of dropped. That, according to Jane, he'd left on business the next day. He deserved it. He had no heart. And if she'd somehow managed to hurt his feelings, maybe it was the wakeup call he needed.

Jeff had been texting her on and off since they'd chatted on her parents' couch, and she wasn't sure what to do about it. Flirting was fun, but did she really want to date him? They were going to the movies in a few hours, so apparently she'd find out.

"Was the post office busy?" she called out.

Jane poked her head into the doorway. "Not too bad. But I just realized I didn't package up the other rush order so I have to go back in a few minutes. I'll stop at Mom and Dad's afterward."

"You going out with Charlie tonight?"

"Yep. To the movies."

Elsie frowned. "What time?" It shouldn't matter, but the thought of Charlie blabbing to Will, telling him she'd been out with Jeff made her uncomfortable. But that was stupid. It shouldn't matter. In fact, maybe it would be better if he knew. Jeff Wickham didn't need to lose any more friendships over Will's interference.

"Why, do you need me for something?" Jane asked.

"No. It's just, I'll be at the movies, too. With Jeff. I doubt Charlie and Jeff will want to share popcorn."

Jane smiled. "Probably not. We're seeing that new romantic comedy about the guardian angels who fall in love while helping their charges fall in love."

"Angelic Encounters?" Elsie tried not to be jealous. Jeff had laughed when she'd suggested it. They were going to see some teenage slasher film instead. The theater only had four screens, leaving few choices.

***

Will strode up the walkway to his family home and pulled out his key. He never stayed long, but it was nice to be somewhere he could truly feel like himself. He opened the door and breathed deeply, taking in the faint smell of lemon-scented furniture polish and the stronger scent of baking bread. Already, he could feel his blood pressure lowering.

"Will, is that you?" Gianna called from the kitchen.

"Yes, it's me." He hurried around to greet her and bent down to give her a hug.

She pressed her cheek to his, but kept her arms out wide. "Sorry, my hands are covered in flour or I'd give you a proper hug."

"Smells good." He looked down at the bread dough she was forming and pinched off a piece. "Are you making this for me?"

"Maybe." She slapped his hand before he could take more. "I don't know how you can eat raw dough. Gross. If you'll wait two minutes, the first two loaves are almost ready to come out."

"Why are you making so much?"

She blushed. "Oh, I was going to take some over to a friend. I hope you don't mind. I'll be back in time for dinner. I'm just dropping it off."

Will put his hand on her arm. "If you have other plans, it won't bother me. I'm a big kid. I can take care of myself."

"No, really. He doesn't know I'm coming so I might be leaving it at the door. But Dallin mentioned the other day how much he liked homemade bread."

"Dallin?"

Gianna wouldn't look him in the eye. "He's on my wheelchair basketball team. And he's been helping me with my shot. Do you know how embarrassing it is to miss the hoop by several feet?"

Will raised an eyebrow. "Last time I checked, helping a girl with her shot was code for putting the moves on her." He couldn't help teasing, but he felt bad when Gianna's face dropped.

"He has a girlfriend."

"I'm sorry, Gianna. That could change though. People break up all the time."

She shook her head. "He's just being nice. And I'm so shy, it's actually easier to talk to him knowing he's off limits. There's another guy I'd like to get to know better if I wasn't so tongue-tied all the time." She wiped off her hands and pulled on oven mitts as the timer went off.

"I'll get that," Will offered.

Gianna shook her head. "You went to all the trouble of having the appliances lowered in here. Let me show off my appreciation."

Will waited and took the piping hot pan from Gianna, and then flipped it over on the table, patting it until the loaf popped out. "So, Dallin is like your practice guy."

"You will not let this go, will you?" Gianna did the same with the second loaf before wrapping it in a decorative towel and sticking it in a basket she'd prepared.

"Looks great. I'm sure he'll love it. Why not send one to tongue-tied guy, too?"

"Will, you are pushing your luck. Besides, I need you to break into that other loaf and taste it, make sure it's okay."

46

Will pulled off a hunk, not bothering with a bread knife, and stuck it in his mouth. What he could taste of it before his taste buds burned off was delicious. "Mm hmm. Do you want me to go with? I could drive." He tried to sound casual about it, but she read between the lines anyway.

"Will, I like driving. Yes, it's a pain to take apart my chair and put it back together every time, but you have no idea how much happier I am knowing I don't have to ask for help. I don't have to wait on anyone except me." She picked up her purse and wheeled her way down the hall, although she let Will get the heavy door to the garage and hold it open for her. "Besides, Caroline's coming to dinner, and she'll be here any minute."

"What?" Will followed Gianna out to the garage. "She invited herself, didn't she?"

Gianna grinned. "I may have mentioned you were coming home for a few days, and suddenly her schedule cleared up. She's bringing me a Chanel purse she doesn't want anymore. I'll make dinner in exchange for a five thousand dollar purse any day."

"I don't want you carrying that around. You'll just be asking to get mugged."

"Aren't you worried about Caroline, then? Her latest purse cost ten thousand."

"Caroline would talk the robber into turning himself in with one of her famous guilt trips. So, no, I'm not worried about her." Will watched Gianna shift her body into the driver's seat and then fold up her wheelchair, popping off the wheels, and placing everything in the seat next to her. He had to admit, she was getting faster and more confident. He handed her the basket and she set it in the seat behind her. His smile dropped when Gianna hit the garage door button to reveal Caroline already parking at the curb outside.

"Make a salad together," Gianna called out as she pulled out of the driveway.

CHAPTER 7 ♥ MOSQUITOS AND WOMEN

Elsie didn't want another bite of over-salted movie popcorn but she kept eating it, every handful a physical reminder that she was still in a movie theater and this was only a scary movie. Nobody was actually dying, despite all the screaming and blood splatter going on. She hated scary movies. Onscreen, a gorgeous actress in a sweaty tank top held up a butcher knife, breathing heavily in a way that best showed off her impressive chest.

"She's going up the stairs," Jeff murmured. "Man, this girl's dumb."

"But if she dies up there, does that mean the movie will be over?"

Jeff rubbed Elsie's knee. "Hang in there. This is the good part. And I promise she doesn't die. She has to be around to make another one next Halloween."

"How comforting." She took another bite of popcorn before handing Jeff the bag. "Keep this away from me."

He took it automatically, too absorbed with what was happening on the screen to even look over. Elsie slid down in the seat and pulled out her phone, going to her email app and checking T-shirt orders. They'd made an awesome ghost graphic, and with Halloween two weeks away, they needed to sell as many as possible while there was still time to ship.

If they'd been watching Angelic Encounters, like Jane and Charlie, there was no way she'd turn to work. After going through her work emails, she scrolled through their social media accounts, responding to anyone who commented on their business page.

Jeff nudged her as loud rock music blared out and the credits started rolling down the screen. "Amazing, huh?"

Elsie looked up. How much time had passed? She put away her phone and shrugged. "Not exactly my kind of movie. How many times have you seen this?"

"I went with Lydia last night. She loved it, but I get the feeling you two don't agree on much."

"No, not much." Strangely, the thought that Jeff had been on a date with her little sister last night didn't bother her. A sign this relationship was firmly planted in the friend zone. Not necessarily a bad thing.

Elsie grabbed her purse and followed Jeff out. He put his arm around her and hugged her to him. "What do you think, ice cream after this?"

Elsie couldn't help calculating out how expensive this date was getting. Dinner, about forty dollars, movie tickets, popcorn and drinks, another forty, and now ice cream? Jeff waved her off when she'd offered to pay for her ticket, reminding her that thanks to Will Darcy, he didn't have his license and she was the one driving them everywhere. It was only fair he treated her to everything else.

But that only made her wonder how he managed to pay for things. Did he have a job? Was it rude to ask? Jeff seemed to be on an extended vacation with Denny, crashing at Denny's cousin's house.

"I could go for a little ice cream, but it's my treat."

Jeff pinned her with a look. "Not a chance. What are you so worried about?"

How could she word this properly? "Jeff, I know you're probably hurting for money right now, and that's fine. I won't think less of you if we have to split the tab. Or maybe do something not so expensive next time."

Jeff opened the door to the theater, leading her out to the parking lot. "You really aren't Lydia."

"Lydia likes to be taken care of, but I'm an independent girl."

Jeff smiled. "Will sent my life into the toilet, it's true. But I'm okay now. I promise."

"Then the ice cream is on me?" Elsie insisted.

Jeff rolled his eyes. "Of course not. I didn't even tell you the best part. Denny and I decided to become day traders, and it's going really well. So, now that you know I have a job, will you quit henpecking me and let me finish this date with my ego intact?" He grinned in the way that made it seem like everything in the world was good.

"All right, big shot. But be warned, I'm ordering two scoops. And possibly fudge sauce too."

***

"Will, darling!" Caroline breezed out of her BMW and jogged up the driveway in her three-inch heels. "What a coincidence we're both in town at the same time. I'm headed to Florida next weekend for a Kappa Sigma reunion. We're all staying in a condo together. It's going to be amazing. Here, be a dear and take this cake dish from me and I'll tell you all about it."

He took the dessert and held open the door for her, silently cursing Gianna for selling him out for a free purse. Personally, he'd always found the purses Caroline carried around to be oversized and old-ladyish, but whatever.

Once inside, they played an awkward version of musical chairs, as everywhere Will sat down, Caroline followed, snuggling into the crook of his arm. And all the while she continued to talk about her stupid trip to Florida until he finally pushed her off and stared her down, ending her boring speech once and for all.

"Caroline, stop this. You know we would never work."

She glanced down at her nails, pretending to study them. "I know, Will. But you don't have to be so prickly with me. You act as if women were mosquitos to be swatted away."

Only some women. He ignored the jibe and took up Gianna's suggestion. "Why don't we go get started on the salad?"

Caroline looked like she was going to continue sulking, but she stood up and followed him into the kitchen, occasionally making jokes about what he might do if their hands accidentally touched while exchanging tomatoes and carrots. Will only smirked. Caroline was a much more interesting conversationalist when she was mad at him.

Gianna returned and took in Caroline's stiff posture and Will's eye roll. She smiled. "Will, would you mind checking my computer while Caroline and I finish up dinner? It's making this funny noise when I turn it on, and I'm afraid the engine thingy is wearing out."

"I'd be happy to." He headed into the den and closed the double doors behind him. Gianna wasn't off the hook yet, but he couldn't help chuckling at her specialized terminology. "Engine thingy," he muttered. Hopefully, this was a pretend problem and not a real one. He might know more about computers than Gianna, but not by much.

He turned her desktop computer on and waited, but everything seemed fine, so he read the news until Gianna came to coax him back to the kitchen for dinner.

"Why did you tell her I was coming home?" he whispered. "I was looking forward to spending some time with you without having to entertain anyone. Oh, and your computer is all 'fixed.'"

"Tell her you're not interested. Why do you play these avoidance games with her?"

"I've told her. Repeatedly. She just insults me and then goes back to wearing me down."

"Then tell her you have a girlfriend. And get one. What about that girl in Meryton?"

The door creaked. "What girl in Meryton?"

Will and Gianna turned back to stare at their eavesdropper. "No one," they said in unison.

***

Elsie's phone buzzed while she was scraping the bottom of her ice cream bowl for one last delicious bite. Jeff had already scarfed his down and was turning his napkin into an origami bird. Seeing her mom's name on the phone screen was not the highlight of the evening. Elsie almost ignored the call, but if it had something to do with Dad, she wanted to know right away. "Hi, Mom."

"Elsie, you must come over here immediately. Collin just showed up in a gorgeous sedan. You have to see this car. And his matching luggage set is to die for. Anyway, we were having pie, and he mentioned his financial advisor wants to see him in a steady relationship with someone sensible and humble, someone who can keep him grounded and away from gold diggers who would rob him blind. And he's asked about you girls. Jane's not answering her phone. I need you to find her, and the two of you must come here and meet him. Make sure you're wearing makeup this time."

"Mom, you should keep your voice down. What if he can hear you?"

"Oh, your father is out back with him, showing him the citrus trees. But you must come soon!"

"I can't right now. I'm out with someone."

Jeff leaned over and tickled her ribs. "That's right you are."

Elsie stifled a giggle and tried to lean out of his reach.

"What is so funny, young lady?"

Mrs. Bennet's hysterical voice only made it harder for Elsie to keep from laughing. "Can't I come tomorrow? I'm sure Collin's tired from traveling."

"He's just fine. And I already told him you were eager to meet him and would be coming right over."

Elsie banged her head on the table in front of her, which only made Jeff laugh harder.

"Are you there, Elsie?"

"I'm here."

"Are you coming?"

Jeff, who could hear the entire conversation, nodded eagerly, mouthing "me too."

"Do you mind if I bring a friend?"

"As long as she's not too pretty. I don't want anyone else competing for Collin's attention."

Jeff batted his eyelashes and pretended to fluff his hair.

Elsie gave him a shove. "Don't worry about that, Mom. We'll be over soon."

***

Caroline studied the computer screen behind Will as if it might have the answer she was seeking. But unfortunately for her, there were no news articles about Will's dating life. She snapped out of it and pasted back on a smile. "Sorry to interrupt. Um, are you two coming in for dinner?" She leaned against the doorway in what she probably hoped was a casual stance.

"Of course we're coming." Gianna nudged Will's arm. "Calorie counting is on hold for tonight. I made lasagna, and Caroline brought her famous chocolate cake. It's to die for."

"Actually, the cake I made this time is gluten-free and packed with antioxidants from all the organic spinach."

52

"Sounds delicious," Will said with more than a hint of sarcasm. He sat down across from Caroline and served up salad to Gianna's plate, and then his.

Caroline's eyes narrowed as she took the bowl from him. "It is delicious, Will. And I'll expect an apology after your second slice."

"Well then, we'll have to save room for dessert," Gianna said, once again playing peacemaker.

Will decided he wouldn't eat a single bite of spinach cake, no matter what. "Don't eat too much, Gianna. I want to take you on in basketball after this."

Gianna grinned. "Fine, but I'm leaving the hoop at eight feet."

Caroline dropped her fork. "Basketball? Will, are you making a joke? That's highly insensitive of you."

Gianna touched Will's hand before he could say something rude in response. "Caroline, I just started playing in a wheelchair league, and Will was so excited for me, he had the ballroom converted to a basketball court."

Caroline's eyes widened in alarm. "Your parents' ballroom? But we had our sixteenth birthday parties in there. Your parents' twenty-fifth anniversary ball…"

Gianna's face dropped, and Will put his fist down on the table a little harder than he meant to, making the silverware jump. "Stop it, Caroline. There won't be any hoity-toity balls held in there again. At least now it's not just an echoing room, collecting dust. Gianna's friends come over and play every week. Besides, from a purely financial standpoint, it's a good renovation, making the space more attractive to future homebuyers." He turned to Gianna. "But that's not why I did it. I'd renovate it again if you suddenly decided you needed an indoor zoo, or a gigantic sewing room, or a replica of the Taj Mahal. I just want you to be happy."

Caroline sniffed, and Will looked over at her, surprised to see she was actually teary-eyed. "I'm sorry. I shouldn't have said anything. It caught me by surprise is all." She gave Gianna a tentative smile. "I don't play, but I'd love to watch the two of you. I assume Will is sitting in a wheelchair for this?"

Gianna nodded. "We keep an extra one."

Will had initially brought up basketball in hopes of sending Caroline home, but she looked so contrite he found he actually wanted her to stay and see for herself. "It wouldn't be the same without you insulting me and hoping I miss all my shots."

Caroline smiled at him. "Of course. But first, my cake."

***

Mrs. Bennet met them at the door and quickly ushered them in, giving Jeff Wickham a wary glance. "This is the friend you wanted to bring along? I thought Jeff was Lydia's friend."

Jeff gave Mrs. Bennet a wide smile and placed a hand on each shoulder. "Mrs. B, I just love spending time with your family. I hope you don't mind my stopping in, but I can go if it's a problem."

Mrs. Bennet fluttered under his steady gaze. "Of course you can stay, Jeff. We're always happy to have friends of Lydia ... and Elsie." She turned to Elsie and smoothed out Elsie's hair. "Collin is in the kitchen chatting with your dad, so go on in. Jane called a few minutes ago and said she was on her way."

Elsie took a deep breath. Joking about the whole thing with Jeff had been fun, but she wasn't looking forward to getting to know Collin again. Or being thrown at him as a potential girlfriend.

"Elsie!" Mr. Bennet's eyes lit up when she entered the kitchen, but then her view of her dad was blocked by a gangly body and a large hand, outstretched to shake hers.

Collin's overly-white smile gleamed. "So good to see you again, Elsie. It's been too long." As he shook her hand, he placed his other hand on top, successfully trapping hers. His hands were super soft, like he'd never had to use them. "You've grown into a beautiful young woman."

She tried not to be creeped out by that statement and let him keep her in his makeshift trap. He finally let go and went in for a hug. Elsie tapped his shoulders and detangled herself from him as quickly and politely as possible. They'd never hugged. Not even when he'd left at the end of the summer fifteen years ago.

She took a step back and glanced behind her at an amused Jeff, watching from the doorway. She pulled on his arm and made him stand next to her. "Let me introduce my friend, Jeff Wickham."

Collin gave him a hearty shake. "What do you do, Jeff?"

Jeff caught Elsie's eye before turning back to him. "I'm a day trader."

Collin's eyes lit up. "Fabulous. Wonderful. So, do you follow a certain software or get tips from someone? How are you picking stocks? I, for one, have always been terrible at it, but I don't have to worry about that now. My financial advisor handles everything. I'm so fortunate to have her."

"Her?"

"Oh yes. Catherine De Bourgh of De Bourgh and Associates. She's a true gem. And she doesn't stop at financial advice. Her motto is 'no detail is too small.'"

Jeff bit back a grin. "She sounds amazing."

Collin missed the teasing in Jeff's voice. "She's extremely thorough. Catherine rearranged my apartment, including my pantry and clothes closet. Everything's so much more spacious and tasteful now. And she knows where all the best restaurants are and recommended I change dry cleaners. Nothing is below her notice."

Mr. Bennet gave Elsie a wink, much too amused by something so ridiculous. "Tell them about your goals, Collin."

And he did. For the next forty-five minutes. By the time Jane arrived, Elsie knew all about Collin's dream to become a life-planner like his mentor, Catherine De Bourgh. He also wanted to create a video series, write a book, and go on tour, teaching people how to own their dreams and reach fulfillment. Somehow he never mentioned the extreme luck that had factored into his recent "fulfillment."

CHAPTER 8 ♥ BLUE EYES AND LIMBO

Will got back from the food pantry and slipped in the door, listening for Gianna. The sound of a basketball dribbling alerted him to her location, and he went into the ballroom, watching her practice for a minute until she realized he was there.

"Are you really leaving today?"

"Yep."

She followed him down to his bedroom where his half-packed suitcase sat on the bed. He threw a few more pairs of clean socks in and took out a few shirts he wanted to leave behind.

Gianna watched him from the doorway. "You're so restless, Will. I hope one day you find whatever it is you're looking for."

Will sighed. "Who says I'm looking for anything?"

She shrugged but decided not to pursue their old argument. "I just miss you when you're gone, that's all."

Will reached out and gave her blonde ponytail a tug. "You're too busy to miss me. Brumhilda will be back any minute now, cracking her whip. And then after killing it in physical therapy, the two of you will pretend you weren't just hating each other and go out shopping, or charity-causing, or whatever it is you two do all day. I'd be a third wheel." *Like I am with Charlie.*

"Brumhilda? Really? I'm telling Becky you called her that."

Will closed the lid of his suitcase and slowly pulled the zipper around. "I hope you do. I'll be too far away for her to doing anything about it."

Gianna wheeled over to his dresser and shut all the drawers he'd left open. "How was the food pantry this morning?"

"The same as always. Busy. I wish I could do more. I feel like we're trying to fix a symptom of something that's so much bigger."

"But that's why we have The Darcy Foundation, Will. There are so many people who have you to thank for their steady job. You can't save everybody."

"I know. Let's talk about something else. How's Dallin?"

Gianna groaned. "No way. Why don't we talk about pizza girl? When are you seeing her again?"

Will picked up the suitcase from off the bed. "Tonight. There's a birthday party for her sister, Jane. The one currently dating Charlie. And he's hosting it."

"Do you have a gift?"

Will's shoulders dropped. "Dang, I'm expected to bring a gift, aren't I? Gift card?"

Gianna started to shake her head, and then shrugged. "That's probably best. But not for too much. You'll make Charlie look bad."

"Ha." Will snorted. "Knowing Charlie, he'll have made a personalized scrapbook for her or created a scavenger hunt ending in a field of roses. Something ridiculous that women find romantic."

"You could use a little tutoring in what's romantic. It's not all ridiculous, you know."

Will checked under the bed and found an errant sock. "Money is romantic. At least to all the women I've dated."

"And that, Will, is exactly your problem."

***

Jane seemed to be having a wonderful time, not at all worried about being the center of attention or mixing family with friends new and old, but Elsie's stomach was a ball of nerves. And that was before Will Darcy walked into the party and locked eyes with her. He looked away first, taking in the boisterous group milling around Charlie's living room.

Her entire family had come, even Mary for the weekend. And of course Collin, still mooching off her parent's hospitality, despite being the richest person in the room. Collin was going on and on about personal fulfillment and life goals again, thanks to her dad's unending encouragement. The whole thing was so embarrassing.

"Will! What took you so long?" Charlie pulled on Will's arm and took him around, introducing him to everyone.

Lydia gave Will a cold stare and turned back to Kat, speaking loud enough for him to hear. "I can't believe Jeff and Denny wouldn't come. As soon as I told them it was at Charlie's house, they made up some dumb excuse. Men and their feuds."

Will looked like he wanted to say something, but Jane came up to give him a hug and he handed her the card he'd been holding. "Happy birthday, Jane."

Her face lit up. "Oh, that's so nice of you. Should I open it now?"

Will shrugged, looking embarrassed. "If you'd like."

She threaded a finger through the lip of the envelope, the noise in the room suddenly down to a small hum. Mrs. Bennet stopped talking to Collin and turned to look over Jane's shoulder.

"A fifty dollar Visa gift card," Mrs. Bennet crowed before Jane even had a chance to read the card. "How generous."

Jane thanked him profusely, ignoring the fact that their mother had snatched the card out of Jane's hand and was showing it around, praising Will's handwriting and thoughtfulness.

When she reached Mary, dressed all in black, Mary tapped the card and sneered. "Money is a poor second to art, love, or time." Upon which she pulled out a notepad, repeating the phrase to herself as she wrote it down.

Somehow, Elsie was sure that line would end up in a café poetry reading sometime soon.

Oh, this was getting worse. Collin, having lost his audience to a birthday card, wedged his way over to Will and put out a hammy hand. "I don't think we've met. I'm Collin Edgewood, life planner and motivational speaker."

Will stared at the hand for several seconds, as if debating what to do with it. Finally, he put a hand to Collin's shoulder instead and looked him in the eye. "And now we've met. If you'll excuse me." He escaped past him onto the back porch and collapsed in a deck chair, running a hand through his gorgeous wavy hair.

"What's with him?" Kat asked.

Elsie let out a long frustrated breath. "I think he finds our family a little overwhelming. I can't say I blame him."

She decided a little fresh air wouldn't hurt her either and went out the front door instead. Her phone buzzed in the front pocket of her sundress and she pulled it out, smiling when she saw it was a text from Jeff. *How's the party going?*

It'd be better if you were here. But there was no use dwelling on that. Charlie probably would have graciously tolerated his presence, but with Will here, there was no way Jeff could have come. It was so unfair.

I still need to get a present for Jane. What kinds of things does she like?

How like Jeff to actually want to put some thought into his gift. Although Elsie had to admit, it'd been awfully nice for Will to get Jane a gift at all. Knowing Jane, she'd use the money on something tangible, but necessary, like a toaster. And then she could look at it every day and think how nice it was of Will to think of her on her birthday. Jane could make anything meaningful. Elsie had never known a more gracious person. *Jane likes unicorns, popcorn tins, mint-flavored cocoa, and word puzzle books.*

A random list only a sister could come up with.

Elsie smiled. *Just trying to be helpful.*

Footsteps sounded on the gravel by the side of the house, and Elsie looked up from her phone, alarmed to see Will approaching. She tucked her phone away and smoothed out her dress, immediately berating herself for doing so.

"Can I join you?" he asked.

"There are no chairs," Elsie pointed out.

"That didn't stop you from coming out here." He leaned against the railing, too close for her liking. "We could walk to the back porch."

She shook her head. "I'm fine."

"You sure? I could go grab two chairs and bring them around."

This guy was such an enigma. Friendly one minute, aggravating the next. And being out here in the dark, just the two of them… Elsie wasn't sure what to think. "I'm okay with standing. I'll be heading inside in a minute."

She glanced through the front window. Everyone was gathering around a limbo stick, the traditional limbo song blaring out of Charlie's speakers. Maybe she wouldn't go inside yet. She did smile to see them lift the stick, letting her dad duck under it first, to great applause. Leave it to her family to pull out such a juvenile game at an adult party. Lydia was next, and Elsie quickly blocked the window with her body and turned back to Will.

"Not a fan of the limbo?" He asked with a twinkle in his eye.

Ah, back to being a condescending tease. This was much more comfortable territory. "Can't say I've ever tried it. You?"

"You couldn't pay me enough."

Elsie raised an eyebrow. "I think that means you have too much money. Or maybe too much pride. Isn't there something you want badly enough that you'd dance under a stick for it?"

He took a step toward her, and she stepped back against the window, alarmed that there was no more room she could put between them. It was the expression on his face, like she'd introduced an idea she'd had no intention of putting there.

"What are you doing?" she asked.

"Are your eyes blue or gray?"

"In this light they could be anything. But usually blue." Why did he care about her eyes? The best thing would be to keep talking. "They're very much like my mom's."

"No, I don't think so."

"That's just because you don't like her."

"Why would that determine whether I think her eyes are like yours?"

"What?" She couldn't concentrate on the conversation. Was he leaning in? Elsie's eyes flickered to his lips without her permission. His cologne was heavenly, probably very expensive, and clouding her judgment. She should run. She should run right this minute. She hated this guy.

He put a hand to her waist, his face now a few inches from hers. "Definitely blue. I can see it now."

A sharp knock on the window broke her trance, and she sidestepped away from Will and opened the front door, escaping back into the party. The sharp change in noise level and brightness left her momentarily stunned, and she almost forgot to check who had been knocking at the window. But there was Collin, waving stupidly to Will, trying to get him to come in.

"I just realized something," he shouted through the glass. "Your aunt is Catherine De Bourgh! What an amazing coincidence. She's my mentor."

He wanted to throttle that goof, Collin, but he also wanted to thank him. He'd been about to kiss Elsie and probably would have been rewarded with a slap. An after-the-fact slap because she was totally sending bring-it signals.

His brain left all logic behind when it came to her, and he had a feeling she felt the same way about him. Pursuing her didn't make sense, and he always did things that made sense. Elsie's family was obnoxious. He didn't know Elsie that well. But she got under his skin in a way no woman had before.

He paced on the front porch, trying to get a hold of himself. Even now, he wanted to go into that stupid party, just to stand next to her. It made no sense.

Charlie found him a few minutes later. "We're about to cut the cake. You should come in, do some mingling. Man, that Collin guy really likes you."

Will rubbed the space between his eyes. "No, he likes my busybody aunt. She's a terrible human being. Although, I have to admire her for turning her ability to get in everyone's business into an actual business."

He followed Charlie back inside and into the kitchen, where at least a dozen people were sandwiched around the island counter. Will ended up next to Charlotte Lucas, glad to find someone whose presence he could tolerate. They bumped shoulders in greeting and then watched Jane try to blow out all twenty-eight candles.

"This tradition was definitely not started by a germophobe," Charlotte muttered.

Will chuckled. "When did you get here? I didn't see you earlier."

"I was walking up while you and Elsie were, um, leaning against the window, and I decided to go in through the back door. You want to tell me what that was all about?"

"Nope."

Charlotte grinned. "That's what Elsie said when I asked her."

He looked across the room and saw Elsie watching them. She immediately dropped her gaze and stepped forward to pick up the serving knife, cutting out pieces of cake with laser-like focus. Nope, he hadn't thawed her yet.

He hated store-bought cake, so he declined a piece and went to his room and shut the door. He'd had about all the Bennet fun he could take and it was better if he separated himself from Elsie. He put some headphones on and got work done, answering emails and going through purchase orders for renovation tasks. He checked an hour later and the noise in the living room was still going strong. Would those Bennets ever leave?

CHAPTER 9 ♥ SHUFFLING

Elsie wasn't sure who had told Collin about their T-shirt business, but he came over bright and early Saturday morning to see for himself. She should have left Collin and his long list of stupid questions on the front porch and never invited him in. Hours later, he was still parked on their couch with no plans to leave.

Elsie decided to withhold food until he returned to her parents, but she should have mentioned it to Jane first. She watched in horror as Jane brought him a sandwich and put him to work packaging and affixing labels to boxes.

There was no way she'd let those go to the post office without double-checking everything, and that would mean time spent reopening boxes and reprinting labels. His help was nothing more than a lot of extra work.

Elsie stepped in front of him. "Collin, my mother just texted and said she's preparing a special lunch for you."

"How nice," he murmured, jamming a T-shirt into a plastic bag and clumsily affixing the adhesive along the side.

Jane gave her a pointed look. Their mother did not text, nor was she making lunch, but that wouldn't keep Elsie from trying.

"Elsie, would you be a dear and hold this box closed while I tape it?" He turned pleading eyes up at her and held out the package.

She reluctantly leaned down and kept the sides closed while he fumbled with their tape dispenser. His hands pressed against hers when he was done, all in the name of securing the tape, and she pulled away, grossed out by his obvious attempt to touch her. The smitten look on his face wasn't helping either.

"You know," Collin said as he tossed the box off the side of the couch. "I could offer you two a generous loan in return for a small percentage of your company. I'd have to run it by Catherine, of course, but it could be lucrative for both of us."

Never. "That's nice." Elsie met her sister's eyes over his head. "Jane? Will you help me with something in the office?"

Elsie stalked down the hall and closed the door behind them as soon as Jane entered. "If I ask him to leave, it'll probably end in a shoving match, possibly with limbs jammed in the door. Please use your sweet persuasion and get him out of here before I murder him."

Jane sighed. "He's harmless. And he's bored at Mom and Dad's house."

"That doesn't mean it's our job to entertain him. Please, please, please. I'll rub your feet. I'll make that peanut brittle you love. Anything."

"Anything?" Jane raised an eyebrow. "Charlie wants to play cards tonight and we need a fourth. Could you get along with Will for one night?"

Elsie immediately pictured Will's intent gaze, felt his hand resting lightly on her hip, remembered the scent of his cologne. "I don't know..."

"Well, I guess I could let Collin try a hand at the T-shirt press. He did ask."

Elsie's eyes widened. "Fine. I'll go with you tonight. What's the worst that could happen?"

Jane let out a little squeal. "Yay."

She went down the hall and with very little convincing, got Collin outside to inspect their tree in the front yard. As a tree expert (Jane's words) he would know exactly why it was weeping sap onto the trunk. He determined the tree had a cold.

While they chatted outside, Elsie called her mother and did some persuading of her own. Soon the special lunch she'd mentioned was a reality, and they sent Collin on his way, thanking him for his help.

***

"Put your computer away, Will. Jane and Elsie will be here any minute."

Will looked up from his spreadsheets and frowned at Charlie. It seemed there was nothing he could do to get Charlie and Jane to stop setting him up with Elsie. Not that he didn't want to spend more time with her, but he knew Elsie resented them dragging her along as much as he resented them worrying about him being a third wheel.

"Why don't you and Jane go out tonight? I have enough work to keep me busy here. And don't try to tell me Elsie would be disappointed. I know that's a lie."

Charlie plopped down on the couch next to him. "You have your whole life to make money, Will. Try doing something besides calculating how rich you are."

"Because playing cards is a much better use of my time." Will snapped his laptop shut. "Speaking of time, what does your boss say? How much longer do you have in Meryton?"

Charlie popped his knuckles one by one and stood up. "Maybe three weeks? They're already talking about a seismic exploration job in San Francisco starting next month so that's probably where I'll go next. But I really like Jane. I don't want to think about leaving right now."

"San Francisco isn't exactly the other end of the world, Charlie."

Charlie let out a long sigh. "You know I don't do long distance relationships. It was a disaster when I tried it with Angela."

"You didn't even try with Angela. You started ignoring her phone calls within days, and the one time you answered, she ended up crying and hanging up."

"That's not true. I did try. It just wasn't meant to be."

"Whatever."

The doorbell rang, and Will rubbed his forehead, trying to rid himself of the headache already forming. Jane and Elsie walked in and sat down, Jane smiling at him, Elsie avoiding his gaze.

Charlie walked over and gave Jane a light kiss before leading her into the kitchen to make popcorn. Elsie put her elbows on her knees and bit her lip, still not looking at him. It took everything in him not to apologize. Though for what, he wasn't sure. Maybe for his existence.

He picked up a deck of cards from the coffee table and absentmindedly shuffled them over and over again. Elsie turned at the noise and watched, somehow fascinated by his simple bridge shuffle.

"How do you do that?"

"This?" He bowed the cards and let them tumble into a neat pile before picking them up again. "It's nothing." He handed her the deck and moved to sit by her on the couch. Her face went from interested to mildly panicked, but she managed to pull it together and give the card deck a sloppy attempt.

"Put your thumbs against the front of each pile. Like this."

She matched his hands, but though she successfully weaved the two piles together, she couldn't seem to pick them back up again to do the bridge part.

"Don't bend them quite so sharply. That's why they're popping back at you and flopping everywhere."

Elsie blew a strand of hair out of her face. "We can't all be perfect like you, Will."

"I sense some mockery there."

She smiled at him. "Just a bit."

"Are you looking for perfection?" He took the cards out of her hands and began shuffling them again, this time using a one-handed method he'd learned from a book of magic tricks when he was ten.

"What do you mean?"

"Do you believe there's one perfect guy out there, and you just have to find him?"

She stared at the moving cards. "Like soul mates? Absolutely not. I think everyone has flaws, and you have to find someone you love so much you're willing to overlook them."

"And have you ever loved anyone that much?" All his questions were clearly starting to bother her, but he liked hearing her answers. He could think of a million things he'd like to ask.

"Jane. But that's a sisterly love. That's different." She folded her arms. "What about you, Will? Are you looking for your soul mate?"

He set down the cards and tapped them with his finger. "I'm looking for someone with certain qualities I admire. Someone with intelligence and courage, a sense of humor. Naturally beautiful, but not vain. Someone kind who could soften my sharp edges."

She smirked at that last part. It was no secret his sharp edges had rubbed her the wrong way on more than one occasion. "Go on. I know there's more to that list."

He leaned forward. "Someone who takes great enjoyment in life, but knows what has value."

She eyed him curiously. "You'll have to explain that last one."

"Some people like everything. And then nothing really stands out as special to them. Take Charlie, for instance." The second the words were out of his mouth he knew how she would take it.

Her brows dipped down. "He doesn't find anyone special?"

No. But he wouldn't say that. "He's just different than me. That's all."

Jane and Charlie came back in with a large bowl of popcorn. "Who's up for charades?" Charlie asked.

"Charades?" Will and Elsie protested at the same time.

Charlie beamed. "Great. Jane and I are a team, and you and Elsie are a team. You two go first. We're doing movie titles." He handed Will his phone, where he already had an online charade generator pulled up and ready to go. Will looked over at Elsie. If she was irritated by his last comment, she was hiding it well. At least this stupid game would be a good distraction.

Will tapped the screen and got the title, *My Fair Lady.* He held up three fingers and Elsie cocked her head in that cute little way she had and looked confused.

"The Three Amigos?"

Will put his hand down. "It means three words, Elsie. Haven't you ever played charades before?"

"No talking," Charlie said, stuffing a huge handful of popcorn in his mouth.

He held up one finger this time and waited.

"First word?" Elsie asked, glancing at Jane and Charlie for confirmation.

"Thirty seconds," Charlie called out.

Will patted his chest.

"My?"

Miraculous. They had one word down. He held up three fingers again and tapped the third one, waiting for her to get that it meant third word. They had about twenty seconds left. He flipped pretend long hair behind his shoulder and did a curtsy.

Charlie roared, which was to be expected. Jane tried to hold in a fit of giggles, but they came bursting out, setting off Elsie.

"I'm sorry," Elsie huffed out between fits of laughter. "Is it *My Best Friend's Wedding?*"

Will sat down on the couch, feeling stupid. Charlie was in so much trouble.

"What was it?" Elsie asked, leaning over.

"It was *My Fair Lady.*"

Charlie howled. Will aimed a kick in his direction and made him get up to take his turn. Anything to take the attention off himself. Jane still couldn't look at him without laughing.

Jane and Charlie seemed to have a charade mind-link because she guessed his title with little effort. Elsie's turn was as disastrous as their first. When he failed to guess *Weekend at Bernie's*, which would have been almost impossible even with good clues, she collapsed on the couch.

"Okay, I would just like to add, that I was brought over here under false pretenses. Jane told me we'd be playing cards, not trying to impersonate dead guys."

"Hear, hear," Will added. He had to admit though, he'd never had so much fun losing. They played a round of Hearts, and Elsie was joking and having fun, up until she got a text message. After she read it, her face dropped.

"Is something wrong?" he murmured while Charlie was dealing out cards.

She shook her head. "I was supposed to meet a friend tonight and forgot about it."

"Charlotte? Invite her over."

"It was Jeff."

Will took the cards in front of him and studied them, trying not to let his disgust show.

"You know, the guy who's not welcome here," Elsie pressed, back to being her combative self.

"No, he's not welcome. He's done irreparable damage to my family, and I can't forgive that."

"You can't forgive an accident?"

Jane and Charlie were waiting with concerned faces. He wasn't having this conversation here, not with Elsie firmly in Jeff's camp.

"Let's just play cards, Elsie. Unless you need to go. No one's holding you here against your will. At least I hope not."

Jane gave a tight smile. "Peanut brittle was on the line. But I'll bribe her into making it some other time. Go, Elsie."

To his dismay, she did. She stood up, stuck her phone in her pocket, and left.

***

Elsie ran all the way back to her house, feeling even worse when she saw Jeff sitting on her porch next to two bags of groceries. She couldn't believe she'd forgotten he was coming over to make dinner, and worse, she'd actually had a good time with Will, someone who wouldn't even let Jeff in the house. It wasn't even Will's house. Man, he could lord over people. And he'd criticized both her card skills and her lack of knowledge about charades. Not to mention his jab that Charlie liked Jane about as much as anyone else.

"Jeff, I'm so sorry. How long have you been sitting here?"

"Only five minutes. Denny dropped me off."

Elsie fumbled with her keys and then beckoned him to follow her in. "Wow, you weren't kidding when you said you wanted to cook for me."

Jeff set the bags of groceries on the counter. "Of course. A gentleman must keep his promises." His mouth twitched. "So, where were you? Dropping off T-shirt packages?"

She very much wanted to lie, and the hesitation caught his attention. He dipped his head down so they were eye to eye.

"I was at Charlie's house with Jane," she admitted.

"Was Will there?" he asked. He was so perceptive. He must have picked up on her guilty expression.

Elsie pulled a glass bottle of balsamic vinaigrette out of one of the bags. "As a matter of fact, yes."

"And does he know you were coming back to see me?"

She nodded. Jeff seemed very pleased to know that. She whacked him in the arm. "Stop acting like such a guy, claiming your territory and all that."

"I just want to protect you from Will. He can be very charming when he wants to be."

"I'm a smart girl. Don't worry about me. Now, what are we doing with all this stuff?"

Jeff directed her to start chopping vegetables while he coated the chicken with the balsamic vinaigrette and threw it in a heated pan. The kitchen smelled amazing.

"Where did you learn to cook?"

Jeff looked over at her and sighed. "Gianna, Will's little sister, taught me. She loves to cook."

"You two must have spent a lot of time together."

"Yes. Hours and hours. But only when Will was off at college. When he'd come home, she wouldn't call me for days." He pulled the chicken out of the pan and put in the chopped veggies, letting them cook in the drippings left in the pan.

"Even now, you two can't be friends?"

"Will would never allow it."

Elsie didn't have any brothers, but she couldn't imagine that kind of relationship was normal, where an older brother controlled his sister's friends. It wasn't right.

CHAPTER 10 ♥ AT THE LIBRARY

Elsie headed to her parent's house early the next morning for her weekly trip to the library. Well, the trip was mostly for her dad. He was supposed to be getting light exercise every day to help with his rheumatoid arthritis, but if Jane or Elsie didn't make him, he was content to sit around the house or in his garden.

It made her sad. All her life he'd been a roofer, constantly tanned from hours out in the sun. Wiry and strong. Now, at only fifty-five, he seemed old.

She slipped in the front door, thankful it was unlocked, and thankful Collin was nowhere in sight.

"He sleeps in," her dad whispered as he shuffled into the room, holding his stack of library books to return.

Elsie smiled. "Well, then let's get out of here before anyone has the chance to demand anything from us."

She waited as her dad slowly made his way to the passenger seat of her car and then she drove the five miles to the library, making sure to park far enough away to give them a good little walk.

Mrs. Bennet, being an impatient woman, had no tolerance for waiting on him to walk anywhere. She brought his wheelchair whenever possible.

"Did you read all those mysteries or do you need to renew any of them?"

He handed them over, and she was happy to carry them for

him without having to offer.

"I read them all," he said. "I'm starting to wonder if I'll run out of library books at some point."

"You have an e-reader, you know. You'd never run out of books on that."

He shrugged. "I like the feel of a real book in my hands."

They stopped to watch two sparrows fighting over a small piece of donut before continuing up to the library doors.

"Maybe we should stop for donuts on the way home," he suggested.

Elsie smiled. She only ate donuts with her dad. She enjoyed the time with him more than the glazed doughy things. When it came to sweets, cookies were more her nemesis.

It was two minutes past opening time, and they waited by the locked door for someone to come to the front. Mrs. Lucas, the head librarian, hurried over and flipped the lock before holding the door open for them.

"Hello, you two. I'm going to head back to finish the book order I started, but if you ring the bell I'll hear it. Oh, and please send Charlotte my way if you see her. She's bringing me a sweater. It always gets so cold in here, and I forgot it this morning."

She left them to their own devices, as she knew Mr. Bennet would require at least an hour of browsing before wanting to check out. Elsie sat at a table and read while he went up and down the fiction aisles, occasionally pulling out a title and reading the back. Elsie was half-way through her own book when a tap on her shoulder alerted her to Charlotte's presence.

"Fancy meeting you here." Charlotte pulled out the chair next to Elsie and plopped down. "I have to be at work soon, but I've been dying to know what's going on with you and Will. I know what I saw the other night at Jane's party."

Elsie put her book down and tried to control the blush she knew must be taking over her face. "That was just Will interrogating me about my eye color." It sounded even more pathetic out loud and she quickly added, "I don't like him, and I doubt he feels anything more than curiosity for me."

"Why don't you like him? I thought he was nice."

"That's because you don't know what he's really like. Jeff Wickham grew up with him, and one day Will Darcy decided Jeff wasn't good enough to hang out with him or his sister anymore.

Will even had charges lobbed against Jeff after a car accident. He's had his license revoked because of it!"

Charlotte didn't seem nearly horrified enough, considering what Elsie had just revealed. In fact, she looked skeptical. "Isn't Jeff the guy always tagging along with Lydia?"

Normally, Elsie wouldn't trust any friend of Lydia's either, but Jeff was more than that. "He's my friend too, and I know he's not lying."

"Well, I like Will. I think you'd be dumb to discount him, just because Jeff thinks he's a snob."

"Will put him in jail!"

"Um, honey, the police put people in jail. It could as easily be Jeff's fault. Or no one's fault. That's why they call it an accident."

Charlotte's cold analysis was not helpful on this subject, and Elsie decided to drop it. "So, what do you think of Collin?"

Charlotte shrugged. "He's very friendly. And I think he was smart to get a financial advisor after winning the lottery. Why do you ask?"

"No reason." Except it only solidified Elsie's feelings about Will. If Charlotte thought Collin was such a great guy, she had no right defending Will.

***

A very tanned Caroline Bingley showed up, ready to take the other guest bedroom in Charlie's house again. Fresh from her college reunion in Florida, she had decided to, in her words, 'recover' somewhere quiet like Meryton.

"And you're still here, Will?" she teased.

"You can't get rid of family," Charlie said, taking the orange juice out of the fridge. "Besides, being by myself is no fun. With you two here, always bickering in the background, I feel right at home."

"What a lovely sentiment, Charlie. Insane, but very kind of you to say." Caroline pulled out her phone. "I have to show you all the pictures from my trip. There's this one single friend of mine I'm dying to set you up with."

"You know I'm dating someone." Charlie handed her a glass of orange juice and poured one for himself.

"Oh, right. I'd forgotten about that. What about Will? Is he dating anyone?" She turned overly innocent eyes on Will and he suppressed an eye roll. Now that she'd overheard Gianna talking about 'that girl in Meryton' she wouldn't be satisfied until she sniffed her out. That was the way Caroline worked. If she ever decided to have a career outside of spending her parents' money, detective work would be an ideal field for her.

"I'm not dating anyone, Caroline."

"He's not," Charlie chimed in. "I think his last girlfriend was … Melanie? Was that her name? That had to have been at least three years ago."

"Two years. She decided to marry her high school sweetheart after he came back from Afghanistan. That's a little hard to compete with."

"Oh, Will." Caroline came over and stood behind his chair, putting her hands on each of his shoulders. "But that was two years ago. It's time to move on."

"I have. I just haven't found someone to move on with. And no, I'm not interested in anyone in your sorority."

Caroline unleashed her hands from his shoulders, much to his relief. "Oh, I wouldn't set you up with Alexandria anyway. She's more Charlie's type. Bubbly and likes to socialize, throw parties. If I ever find a beautiful shut-in who enjoys dry humor and long silences, I'll throw her your way."

"Sounds perfect."

Despite Charlie's reminder that he was already dating someone, Caroline started showing him photo after photo of her old roommates, along with a stream of stories to go with them. Will took that as his cue to leave, preferably to somewhere Caroline would never follow. He'd noticed the town library the other day and decided commandeering a back table to get some work done sounded just right. He wolfed down the last few bites of his toast and excused himself to go shower.

***

Elsie hadn't seen her dad in a while, so she stood and stretched before wandering down the mystery aisle and around to the non-fiction section. Hmm. Nowhere in sight. Maybe he was with Mrs. Lucas. She headed to the front desk and froze as she saw Will Darcy sitting at a small table by the window with her dad, having what looked like a nice chat.

They hadn't spotted her yet, and she ducked behind a bookshelf as she drew closer.

"Oh, Elsie's always loved books. She used to check out *The Babysitter's Club* series one by one. She was a slow reader at first, but she stuck with it until she could devour a book in a few hours. She and Charlotte even started their own babysitter's club. Then they extended into dog walking, and car washes, and catching crickets for Mr. Garcia's pet lizards. She's always wanted her own business. Some people have that drive, you know?"

Elsie pressed a hand to her forehead. Her dad was going on about her cricket catching business? She wasn't sure whether to interrupt or wait for a less embarrassing moment.

"I know exactly what you're talking about, sir. It's a rare thing these days."

Sir? Why was Will calling him sir?

Will sighed. "I've seen many intelligent people waste their lives, while people less capable go on to do amazing things because they want it badly enough. They aren't afraid of a little failure."

Elsie wondered if she'd just been relegated to less capable and less intelligent in his story and decided it was time to interrupt, before her dad brought up more fun anecdotes. After all, he hadn't mentioned her success in overcoming bedwetting at age six or the time she'd almost drowned because someone dared her to jump off the high dive.

She stepped out, pretending to be surprised to see them sitting there. "Oh, hello, Will. I didn't know you were here."

A shiver went through her as his eyes took her in, as if seeing her in a new light. She wasn't sure if his gaze was smug or appreciative. Maybe there was a little of both. Why had they been talking about her anyway?

"Come sit down, Elsie." Her dad patted the chair next to him, and she took the seat, wondering when Will would stop looking at her. His handsome face irritated her. She didn't want to admire anything about someone like him.

"Did you find anything good to check out?" she asked.

Her dad showed her his stack of books. "I'm still looking for the second book in the series. I need to go ask Mrs. Lucas if someone else has checked it out. Oh, there she is."

He groaned as he stood and slowly shuffled over to the front desk. Elsie watched him go, wondering if it would be rude to abruptly get up and follow.

"I'm sure you want your table back." She started gathering up the books her dad had left behind.

Will put a hand out and covered hers. "Leave them. I don't mind sharing."

His touch stirred feelings in her that led to even stronger ones, like panic. She dropped the books and sat back, crossing her arms in front of her. "What are you working on?"

"Just going over bills. Checking the totals before I pay the subcontractors."

He turned his laptop around, showing her an invoice for repairs. The total was less than two-hundred dollars, but he had his calculator app up and she could see the total in the box.

It made sense a rich guy like him would be the type to double check every cent that left his care.

He went back to punching in numbers, and she tried in vain to get through one of her dad's mystery novels. She was glad she'd left her romance novel in the back. She could only imagine what Will might think of it, though it wasn't one of those trashy bodice rippers that Charlotte liked to read.

She looked over at her dad, but he was still deep in conversation with Mrs. Lucas.

"How many invoices do you have to get through?"

He glanced up. "About forty."

"So, you'll be doing this all day. How often do you find something that doesn't add up?"

"It's not just about making sure they add correctly. I want to know what they spent my money on. If you don't question at least some of these charges, they assume you'll rubber stamp anything and start cheating you blind."

She leaned forward, finally feeling like he was showing his true colors, the paint only Jeff brushed him with. "Do you really think everyone will cheat you blind when given the opportunity?"

"Not purposefully. But if they know they might be questioned on it, they'll make sure the expense is justified. Everyone needs accountability in their work, Elsie. Think of it like teenagers working at an ice cream parlor. If the boss is never there, they start sitting on the counters eating ice cream and giving out free scoops to their friends. They're not robbing the place, but they aren't working very hard either."

"And if you're the boss? What keeps you or me accountable?"

He stared into her eyes. "The gnawing fear that you could lose everything if you royally screw up. Don't tell me you don't feel that occasionally with your business."

She couldn't say she'd never felt it. That fear had led her to repackage every box Collin touched.

Who was Will Darcy, really? He could have belittled her or dismissed her, but here they were discussing business together as if her small pile was just as important as his massive pile of money.

CHAPTER 11 ♥ CREEPY COLLIN

As Elsie walked her dad up to his door, they were met by a smiling Collin and her beaming mother.

"Elsie, dear. Collin here has graciously offered to take you to lunch so you two can spend some time getting to know one another." Her mom's head tilted toward Collin, her smile becoming more of a threat than an expression of joy as she saw Elsie's reaction.

Elsie did not want to go anywhere with Collin. His endless talking gave her a stress headache. She looked to her dad, hoping for an ally.

"She likes Mexican food," he said, patting Collin on the shoulder. "Have fun."

Turning to Elsie, he whispered. "I could use a little peace and quiet in my garden. Just for an hour or so, if you don't mind."

What was the last few hours then? She dropped his library books in an unceremonious heap on the carpet and followed Collin to the garage. The goon had been afraid to leave his Mercedes Benz on the street, and so had forced her parents to park their Buick outside during his visit. Collin swept past her and opened his passenger car door. "Your carriage awaits, my lady."

It was a nice gesture with a cheesy delivery, made worse when he shut the door on her ankle. She growled in pain and pulled out her phone, quickly texting Jeff.

Help! Save me from a bad date w/ Collin

Collin got in and turned the engine, letting the beast roar to life. He looked over to see if she appreciated the power of a luxury car. She'd appreciate it more if he'd check his mirrors. He backed out with barely a glance and then sped down the street towards town, all the while explaining how he'd purchased his baby from a car collector, and the type of car wax he liked on it, and many other details she didn't care about.

Her phone vibrated with a response.

Wish I could. Just enjoy it. I'll want details...

Very helpful of him.

She interrupted Collin's rambling. "Um, Collin, I have a lot of work to get done at home. I appreciate lunch, but I need to get back as soon as possible. Jane will be waiting on me. In fact, I should call her and check in."

Collin reached over and covered her phone with his hand. "Elsie, I'm a man of details. I already called Jane, and she assured me she could spare you for a few hours."

Jane!

"There's a reason I've gone to all this trouble. I have limited time and goals which must be achieved while I'm here. You, dearest, are a part of that if you'd like to be. But we can discuss it over lunch."

He pulled into the parking lot of Domingo's and got out before Elsie could put together a response. What was he talking about? Why was he calling her dearest? And all the while she couldn't help imagining how much Jeff would enjoy this story later. Like he was some invisible observer to her strange date.

Collin got her door, and she made sure to be out of the way when he closed it this time. She followed him into the restaurant, cringing as he loudly bantered with the hostess, a girl maybe sixteen who bit back a laugh when he asked for their finest table.

Elsie sat down in the booth first and Collin followed, cozying right up next to her. She shifted over and put her purse down between them, thankfully settling that skirmish once and for all.

"Collin, it's been nice having you visit, but I don't see how I can be a part of your future plans. I'm not really into self-help and goals and all that."

His eyebrows rose. "Oh, but you are. I told Catherine De Bourgh all about you last night, and she thinks your little business is a good sign you have the humility and independence necessary for a relationship with me."

Elsie picked up her menu, opening it up like a shield between them. "A relationship with you? Like a business relationship? Collin, I already have a partner in Jane. I don't want your money. We're good. I promise. Do you like enchiladas? They have a great red enchilada here."

He lowered the menu and grinned. "Say that again."

"What?"

"Say you don't want my money. It's so refreshing. I could just kiss you." He pulled down her menu and leaned in with puckered lips, his hands reaching for her.

Elsie scooted back and slid out the other side of the booth, dragging her purse with her. "Actually, I'm not hungry." She flipped around and ran right into a waiter with a tray full of food. Dishes and tacos flew everywhere, landing with a deafening clatter.

She bent down and started picking up pieces of broken plate. "I'm so sorry. I'm so sorry." This was a nightmare. She picked up half a taco shell and a wedge of lime and put it back on the tray, her hands shaking from adrenaline and humiliation.

The waiter's face went from irritated to sympathetic. "I got this, ma'am. It's okay. Just sit back down and enjoy your meal."

That was the last thing she wanted to do. Somewhere behind her, Collin was demanding to speak with a manager. She flipped around and stared him down. "We do not need a manager, Collin. Be quiet for once. That was totally my fault. I'd like to go home now, and then I think you should pack your things and go home as well. Let my parents have their garage back. Sometimes goals have to change. That's part of life. Cross me off whatever list you have me on."

Collin's mouth flapped open and closed like a fish. Speechless. That had to be a good sign. Maybe the message was finally getting through.

"I'll wait for you by the car." She opened her purse and took out a twenty dollar bill. On the way out she handed it to the hostess and apologized for ruining someone else's food.

"Hold on." The hostess ran after her and pulled something out of Elsie's hair. It was a piece of shredded lettuce.

***

"We have plans tonight."

Charlie had that gleam in his eye, and Will reluctantly closed his laptop and waited to see what his friend was talking about. Hopefully, whatever it was would be better than trying to get work done while Caroline attempted to engage him in conversation. But then, that was probably why Charlie was so confident Will would accept.

"Three words. Haunted Corn Maze."

Will dropped his head in his hands. "Really? What are we, fifteen?"

"Elsie's coming along."

"Who?" Caroline ducked her head into the kitchen and folded her arms. "Why a corn maze, Charlie? You know I'm allergic to corn."

"And teenagers dressed up as zombies," Will added.

Caroline nodded. "Yes. I'm definitely allergic to those." She glanced back at Charlie. "Who's going?"

Will had warned him about Caroline's attempt to sniff out his mystery girl, which had forced Will to admit to Charlie that yes, he'd been talking about Elsie with Gianna, and yes, he was, in a totally hypothetical way, interested in someone like her. Charlie had reacted as expected, with enough excitement to embarrass Will for the rest of his life. But he did promise to try to keep Caroline in the dark.

"Oh, Jane and I, and her little sister. We throw her and Will together so neither of them has to be a third wheel. Though they both seem to hate each other."

Will nodded. "We do. It's awkward."

And yet, now that he knew she was coming he was filling with an excitement he knew he'd have to tamp down in front of Caroline. There was no earthly reason why he should be excited about a corn maze.

"What do you hate about her?" Caroline asked, sitting next to Will and staring him down.

He took a moment to think. "She's judgmental, and rude, and she works at a disgusting pizza place in town." All true, and yet he was starting to not care about any of those things. After all, he was judgmental and rude, too.

"What does she look like?" Caroline's eyes narrowed. She could sniff out a lie from a mile away. And Will rarely lied. He usually had no problem telling anyone what he thought about them.

"Oh, plain brown hair. Blue eyes. Fairly ordinary." He shouldn't have mentioned her eye color.

Charlie gave Caroline's chair a soft kick. "Give it a rest. What are you, the dating police?"

Caroline had the sense to look embarrassed and got up, heading over to the sink. "Who didn't rinse out their bowl?"

Charlie admitted to the crime and went to rectify the situation.

***

"I am not going anywhere tonight, and I'm not very happy with you right now." Elsie threw her romance book across the room for good measure, though it landed safely against the couch and slid to the floor.

"I'm not speaking to you, or Mom, or Dad, and if Collin so much as breathes in my direction, he'll get a stiff kick in the you-know-where."

Jane folded her arms and calmly waited. "Are you finished?"

"Are you kidding me? I told Collin in no uncertain terms to GO HOME, and his response was that he wasn't leaving Meryton without me. I truly think he saw it as the most romantic response possible. And then he leaned in to try to kiss me. Again. But we were parked in Mom and Dad's driveway this time so I gave him a firm push back, and he whacked his head on the driver side window. I thought that was the moment he'd get it, but Mom texted as I was hightailing it back here and said he wants to have a meeting with them and me, and I told her she was dreaming. He can go ahead and sue me for assault and I'll see him in court. And then when I come in and tell you I've had an epically bad day you respond with, 'wanna go to a haunted corn maze?'"

Jane took a cautious step toward her and put her arms around Elsie for a hug. "So, this is you not speaking to me?"

"You told him I was free for lunch!"

Jane patted Elsie's back. "I didn't know lunch would come with a marriage proposal."

"It wasn't a proposal," Elsie murmured into Jane's shoulder. "More like a business meets pleasure kind of arrangement."

"Oh, gross. Stop, I can't…" Jane covered her mouth, but her laughter escaped anyway and Elsie finally gave in and laughed with her.

"So, you guys need me as Will's date again?"

Jane tilted her head. "This was Charlie's idea. He thinks Will might have a thing for you and I happen to agree. After you left the other night, Will was never quite the same."

"He knew I was with Jeff. That's all."

"You haven't talked about Jeff in a while. Is everything okay with that?"

Elsie sighed. "I get the feeling he's avoiding me. I don't know why, though."

"Well, he's only here for a short while, right? Just like Charlie." Jane's smile dropped and she walked down the hall towards her bedroom. Elsie followed.

Jane went to the closet and started flipping through possible outfits. "Charlie won't give me a firm date of when he's leaving. He doesn't want to talk about it. I think he just doesn't like to talk about unpleasant things, period. Elsie, I'm starting to fall in love with him and we have no future."

"You don't know that for sure." Elsie put back the flowered shirt Jane was holding and pulled out a red-checkered one. She fingered it, coming up with a stupid idea. Something she'd likely regret, but would hopefully irritate the heck out of Will Darcy. And squelch any romantic ideas he might have, however misguided.

"Jane, let's go have fun tonight. No worrying about guys, or possible legal action, or meddling parents. Do you still have those jean overalls?"

Jane looked back, puzzled. "Yes, but, why would I wear those?"

CHAPTER 12 ♥ AT THE DENTIST

"Your dates are here," Caroline practically sang. She seemed awfully chipper to be sending them off.

Will went to the door and stared, his eyes moving from Elsie to Jane and back to Elsie. Jane had straw sticking out of the top of her overalls and they were both wearing straw hats and plaid long-sleeved shirts. Elsie's button nose was painted brown and her cheeks had two circles of red blush. He wanted to go tug on one of her pigtail braids, but her expression was daring him to try something, to say something, so he refrained.

Charlie came up from behind and laughed out loud. "Girls, you look amazing! Is this a dress-up thing? Should Will and I go change?"

"We're fine, Charlie." Will stepped out onto the porch, but Charlie didn't follow.

"Hold on, I want a picture. Stand with the girls, Will."

Charlie lifted his phone, but Caroline took it out of his hands. "Go get in the picture. I've got this."

Will put an arm around Elsie's waist, and the electric charge between them started up again. He heard her take a deep breath as his fingers pressed lightly against her hip.

He almost forgot to smile as several flashes went off.

"Hold on. That girl had her eyes closed. In both." Caroline eyed Elsie with thinly veiled irritation and then took a few more pictures before handing the phone back to Charlie.

"I think you look cute," he whispered before moving his arm.

She blushed and turned away, heading for the car. They were taking Charlie's Jeep, and Jane got in the passenger seat, leaving Will and Elsie to sit in the back.

"Have you been to one of these before?" he asked.

"Oh, yeah. But not for years. What about you?"

"Plenty of haunted houses, but never a corn maze."

"Well, a family runs this one and every year they have a new theme. And since they refuse to repeat themes, they keep getting weirder."

Jane turned around from the front seat. "Last year was bridal party. They had undead bridesmaids in matching dresses and a wedding cake covered in cockroaches. Lydia was telling me about it. She goes every year."

Jane turned back around and took Charlie's hand that was resting on the console. He lifted her hand to his mouth and kissed the back of it. Charlie made dating look effortless. Will couldn't remember a time Charlie had ever been nervous around a girl.

And here sat Will, buzzing with nervous energy. "So, what's this years' theme?" he asked Elsie.

"At the dentist. I checked online a few minutes ago." She leaned over to show him her phone, and her straw hat bumped him in the jaw.

"Oh, sorry." She took it off and placed it on her lap before running her hands over her two braids to try to smooth them out. There was one strand that was sticking up in a loop, and he reached out, pausing when her eyes began to question him.

"Can I fix one spot?"

She nodded, her gaze never leaving his face.

He gently tucked the errant strand back into the braid, aware his breath was landing on her forehead as he did so. He forced his hands away and sat back.

"So," she stammered, "I imagine we'll be listening to the sound of drills and people screaming and stuff."

"How nice."

"Yes." She stared at him, her eyes even more brilliant when outlined with silly eyelash lines.

***

Why couldn't she feel this way around someone nice, like Jeff? No matter how much she told herself Will was arrogant and unforgiving, it didn't seem to matter. She responded to him like someone with a huge crush, and that was ridiculous. She hadn't known him long, for one. And what she'd gotten to know of him hadn't been all that favorable.

This was not a date, and she was not a love-sick teenager. She could handle this.

Charlie pulled into the dirt parking area and they all got out and walked up to the ticket booth. Inside, an undead dental hygienist sat at a cash register and held out waivers for them to sign, saying they wouldn't punch anyone or sue if they got hurt. Several worn down toothbrushes tinged with red sat in a jar with the pens. It was the grossest thing ever.

"I actually enjoy going to the dentist," Will murmured.

"I bet you've never even had a cavity." Elsie nudged him out of the way so she could pay for her own ticket. Because this was not a date.

He stepped up to pay after her, giving her a wary look. "I've had a cavity or two. Do you insist on paying your portion on all your dates?"

Jane and Charlie were listening so she bit back the words she'd been repeating in her head and gave a small smile. "I thought this was a group activity."

The sound of a drill started up and several people screamed in the distance. Jane gripped Elsie's arm. "I hate that noise."

"Jane, be reasonable. It's just a power tool. And look at that, they have a spider web made entirely out of dental floss." Elsie put a finger out and touched it. A black spider flew down from the top and she jumped back, laughing. It probably had a motion sensor attached. Ingenious. She looked over to find Will watching her. He did that a lot, but she didn't want to think about that right now. She'd been hoping he'd be so embarrassed by her costume that he wouldn't even acknowledge her.

Charlie put an arm around Jane and together they walked towards the opening to the maze. Elsie and Will followed. She stuck close to him, but not too close. It was better to not show fear at places like this. They picked on you when you did. And she wasn't scared yet. More like on alert. Hokey Halloween costumes didn't scare her, but she'd never liked the rustle of corn stalks in a night breeze.

Three steps in, and she moved a little closer to Will. No use tripping on the roots at the edges that stuck out of the ground like skeleton hands. Her shoulder bumped against his, and she went ahead and looped her arm, holding onto his bicep. That way he wouldn't get any ideas about holding hands. He smelled good. Like aftershave and cinnamon gum. Under his sleeve, she could feel the warmth radiating off him.

They hadn't reached anything scary yet, but she knew it was coming. She gripped Will a little harder and forced herself to relax. And then a hand reached out of the corn and grabbed Charlie's calf, sending him down into the dirt. Jane screamed and took off running. Charlie scrambled up and sprinted after her.

Will glanced at Elsie and took a cautious step forward. They were almost to the spot where Charlie had been grabbed. But instead of a hand reaching out, a giant dude in bloody scrubs jumped in front of them, brandishing a drill. A beat up Craftsman with no drill bit in it. Unless he lobbed it at her head, it was not a real threat. A laugh bubbled out of her and once she started, she couldn't stop. The guy glared at her and headed back into the corn. Will turned her to face him.

"What is so funny?"

She laughed harder. "I don't know. Maybe I'm too old for this."

"Well, come on. Let's go see what else your sick sense of humor finds funny."

They jogged together, stopping when the path opened up to a mock waiting area, with beat up old couches draped in fake spider webs and inhabited by skeletons reading newspapers. A tiny skeleton boy in a ball cap kneeled at a wood coffee table covered in dusty toys. One skeleton was hunched over a wastebasket. Green slime oozed over the sides. As Elsie came closer to look, a zombie in scrubs jumped up from behind the couch and growled, reaching out for her. She stumbled backward, and Will caught her under the arms before she fell. She twisted around and hid behind him, but the zombie had already ducked down again. More people were running up the path.

"You can come back out now," Will whispered over his shoulder, laughter in his voice.

Elsie unleashed her hands from his waist. "That's what I get for trying to inspect slime."

They grinned at each other and turned to watch an incoming

group of teenagers get their own zombie scare. Elsie resumed her position on Will's arm. If anyone was going to try to grab her leg tonight, he'd be going down with her. Or at least, that was the story she was going with. Those were not butterflies dancing inside at his nearness, just nerves.

They walked on until there was a break in the path. The teenagers had gone right, so they went left.

"We are never going to find Jane and Charlie," Elsie said.

"I know."

There was rustling in the leaves up ahead to their right, and they both froze.

"I know it's stupid to be scared," Elsie whispered.

"Let's run anyway. Come get on my left side." When she was in position, Will took her hand and squeezed. "Ready?"

She nodded, and they took off, both dodging as a girl drooling blood onto a dental bib tried to grab them.

They eventually slowed when they came to another fork.

"Which way?" Will asked. To their left, the sound of a drill started up, followed by screaming. "Right it is."

He still had a hold of her hand, and she debated whether to pull away. Holding hands signified things she did not want with Will Darcy, and she definitely did not want to send him that message. She gently pulled her hand out and put it back in the crook of his arm.

"Elsie, I—"

"There you two are!" Charlie said, as he and Jane came running up, out of breath. "The exit is up ahead. Follow me."

***

Will had been about to apologize, but maybe it was better to leave things unsaid. Maybe he shouldn't have taken her hand, but if not here, then where? If he hadn't been such a jerk when they'd first met … and again when they ran into each other the second time. Yeah, he was an idiot. He liked having the upper hand too much. Always had. And he wasn't used to caring what people thought of him. Those who knew him well liked him despite his prickly nature. Maybe it was time to stop seeing that as a good thing.

They reached the end of the maze, which was right next to the entrance. There were more people now and more employees in costumes. Several guys dressed like vampires walked around handing out wax teeth candy. A teenager with strong body odor bumped into Will's shoulder and cussed at him.

"Definitely time to go," Elsie said. "The crowd changes around this time of night."

"Are you guys hungry?" Charlie asked.

Jane smiled. "Starving."

Charlie glanced around for his Jeep. "Someone at work was talking about this great Mexican place today. It's called Domingo's."

Will felt Elsie tense next to him. She was still gripping his arm, thanks to the crowds milling around them. "Not Domingo's."

"Why not?" Jane asked. "I like that place, and I haven't been there in ages."

Elsie turned to look at her. "I ate lunch there today."

Jane's face registered something only the two of them understood. "Oh. We'll think of somewhere else then."

Will wanted to ask her about it, but his attention was arrested by a familiar head of hair, skulking off to a dark corner with a girl. The girl's hands went up around his neck and they started making out. It was definitely Jeff, but he wasn't sure about the girl. She kind of looked like that annoying little sister of Elsie and Jane. He glanced back at Elsie, and she'd noticed his distraction. She was peering in the direction he'd been studying.

He positioned his body to block her view. "So, not Mexican food and not pizza. What sounds good?"

"Burgers?"

His brain was going a mile a minute, the indecision of what to do killing him. "How old is your youngest sister?"

"Lydia? She's eighteen. Why?"

"Oh, just trying to learn more about you." Eighteen. Not underage, but definitely not old enough to be skulking around with the likes of Jeff Wickham.

He stopped walking and pulled away from Elsie. "I think I dropped something. I'll meet you all at the car."

They looked puzzled, but nodded and went on ahead. He dashed back to the spot where he'd seen the sister, but she and Jeff were no longer there. Too many people milled around, talking, laughing, shoving each other, screaming. He'd about given up when he spotted her. It was the armful of bracelets that alerted him. Jeff wasn't with her. Even better.

"Where's Jeff?" he asked as he walked up.

"Why would you want to know?" She eyed him suspiciously. "He's too old for you. You need to be careful. He's a bad influence."

She stiffened, looking offended. "I'm eighteen, thank you very much. I don't need dating advice from you." Her face softened as she spotted someone over his shoulder, and Will turned to see Jeff walking up. Jeff's expression turned wary when he recognized Will. And he had reason to be wary.

Will stuck a finger in Jeff's chest. "Messing around with someone fresh out of high school. Real classy, Jeff."

Jeff glanced at Lydia, who was watching them, and his expression morphed into the charming façade he often used to manipulate people. "Our relationship is none of your business, Will. And I'd appreciate it if you'd stop trying to ruin my life. Just when I'm getting my life back together, you show up and try to bring me down again. How dare you insult Lydia by insinuating something sinister is going on here? We're just on a date."

Once again, Jeff, with his silver tongue, had twisted the situation to make himself look good. Some things never changed. Will was not always good with words and they failed him now. It wasn't really his business, except knowing she was better off without him. He gave up on talking to Jeff and instead turned to Lydia.

"You're welcome to come with me and go home with your sisters. I won't say anything to them. They're waiting in the car. I told them I dropped something."

She glared at him and went to stand by Jeff. "I'm staying."

CHAPTER 13 ♥ SECRETS TO KEEP

"Did he say what he dropped?" Jane asked. "We could have gone with him to look."

"Let's all go." Charlie reached for his door handle just as Will jogged up and got in the backseat.

"Sorry guys. Did you decide where we're eating?"

"The diner," Elsie said, studying him. Will was nervous about something. "Did you find what you were looking for?"

He paused and scratched the back of his neck. "No, but it's okay. It was a cheap watch."

Wow, he was a terrible liar. That was unexpected. And he definitely had not been wearing a watch earlier, but she didn't say that and neither did Charlie or Jane.

What possible reason could he have had to return alone? Did he go back for that surly teenager? Will didn't look like he'd been in a fight. She studied his face and then glanced down at his knuckles, but he looked the same as before, except he was staring straight ahead with the strangest expression.

"Are you okay?" she whispered.

He met her eyes. "I'm not sure. I'm worried about someone. Well, to be honest, I'm worried about several people."

"Do these people have names?"

He cracked a small smile. "Yes."

But he didn't follow up with any names. Elsie sat back and folded her arms. Why was she trying to unravel the mystery of him anyway?

At the restaurant, they all shared a booth and Charlie regaled them with several funny stories of him and Will at prep school. They'd met in the fifth grade, with Caroline a grade younger. Charlie described himself as the class clown and Will as a serious rule-follower. No surprises there.

"My parents are so disappointed in me," Charlie said, playing with a sugar packet. "All that money they spent on my education, and I'm basically a construction worker with a fancy degree. But I like what I do. Making new friends in new places."

Jane's smile grew a little tight, and Elsie wondered how Charlie could be so clueless. She glanced at Will, who also looked uncomfortable. Whatever had been bothering him must still be on his mind.

"What do your parents think about what you do, Will?" she asked.

Will and Charlie exchanged looks before Will answered. "My parents are gone. My mom died of cancer when I was eighteen, and my dad died in a plane crash four years ago."

Elsie felt terrible, though there'd been no way of knowing. "I'm sorry. That must be so hard."

The waiter came with their food, and Elsie stared at her burger, no longer as hungry to eat it. No wonder Will had been so protective of his sister. It didn't excuse it, but it did explain why he was the way he was.

"Eat." Will nudged her arm. "It was a reasonable follow-up question, Elsie. And yes, my father was also disappointed by my career choice. He wanted me to go to law school and eventually become a politician. I chose business school instead."

"I could see you as a politician," Elsie said, picturing Will sitting in Congress, wielding power and influence.

"Then you don't know me as well as you think." Will picked up his fork and took a bite of pot roast. "Huh, this isn't bad."

***

Elsie went home after dinner, while Jane stayed late to watch a movie. Will didn't want to interrupt the two cuddling on the couch, but the other worry he'd had ever since seeing Jeff with Lydia was how Elsie might feel about it.

Was he secretly dating them both? The images that filled his mind drove him out of his room and over to the couch.

Charlie looked up at him and paused the TV. "I thought you hated this movie. You coming to watch with us?"

Will shook his head. "Can I ask you something, Jane?"

"Of course." She sat up straighter and looked at him with wide innocent eyes.

"Is Elsie dating Jeff?"

She and Charlie both grinned, not realizing how serious the question was to him. If Jeff was cheating on Elsie with her little sister, she'd be heartbroken.

Jane twirled a lock of her blonde hair. "They're just friends. She said she realized the chemistry wasn't there early on."

One less worry, but it only made him feel marginally better. Elsie had the sense, even if it was only subconsciously, not to get involved with Jeff, but her little sister clearly did not.

He should lay it all out, letting them know what Jeff's influence did to people, but that involved revealing Gianna's fall into alcohol addiction and the fights she'd had with Dad before he died. She was a different person now, and it was something he couldn't bring himself to share, not even fully with Charlie and Caroline. They knew Jeff had caused the car accident, but they didn't know Gianna had been just as drunk that night.

"Jeff hangs out with your sister, Lydia. Is that right?"

Jane shrugged. "I think so. But she has a lot of friends. They come and go."

"What about boyfriends? Jeff is a lot older than her."

"Unfortunately, that's not a new thing. Her first boyfriend was college-age. My parents took her phone when they found out, and that was like a death sentence. Lydia broke up with the guy just to get her phone back."

Interesting. Maybe she'd tire of Jeff all on her own. If he pushed this, it could make her stick to him harder. Maybe it was better to leave it alone. One more secret to keep.

CHAPTER 14 ♥ JUST FRIENDS

Elsie's shift at the Pizza Palace was almost over, but she couldn't help watching the clock anyway. So far she'd been chewed out over the phone by a customer who thought there was not enough pepperoni on her pizzas. Then she had to clean up after a food fight between two unruly kids while listening to their mother scream at them. More helpful than screaming would have been asking the kids to help, but after the mom finished the lecture, they all got up and left.

The bell over the door jangled at five minutes to close, and Elsie tensed up and then relaxed at the sight of Jeff smiling at her.

"Long night?"

"The longest."

He leaned against the counter. "Would you rather go home and veg, or do you want some company? I thought we could try out those swings at the park down the street." He put his finger to his lips. "I borrowed Denny's car to get here. You're not going to turn me in to the cops, are you?"

"Jeff, your license is revoked. That's serious stuff. The cops around here don't have a lot to do, so watch out. But yeah, I'd love to hang out with you. Give me about twenty-five minutes to mop and close up the register. Meet you there?"

"Of course."

The rest of her shift moved much quicker, knowing she had something to look forward to. She waved goodbye to Gerald in the parking lot and drove over to the playground, parking behind

Denny's car.

Jeff was sitting on a swing waiting for her, and she claimed the one next to him. It had been years since she'd sat on a swing. Jeff pushed back and pumped his legs, and she took off to try to match his pace. Despite the chains digging into her hips, it was as fun as she remembered. The breeze in her face, the rush of arching straight down and then going up again, even the creaking brought back happy memories. The starry sky only added to the magic.

Jeff laughed. "You have the goofiest grin on your face."

"Hush, you. I'm having a moment here."

She was starting to get out of breath though, so when Jeff slowed down and came to a stop, she did too.

He leaned in and put his hand on her cheek. "Maybe we could have a moment too," he whispered.

What? It wasn't until his lips were a hair's breadth away that she recovered from shock and pulled out of his reach. "Jeff, you know we're just friends, right?"

He shrugged, looking disappointed, but not hurt. "We never set that in stone, did we?"

"I guess not." She pushed off and swung lightly back and forth, needing something to do with the nervousness inside her. Plus, the movement meant they could break the awkward staring contest that had started.

She had not expected him to put a move on her, but maybe that was only because she figured he felt the same way about her that she did about him.

"Is it because of Will?" he asked softly.

Yes. The answer immediately popped into her head, and she just as soon dismissed it. So she hadn't recoiled when Will Darcy had almost tried to kiss her. It didn't mean anything.

"No, of course not."

"You paused."

"No, I didn't." She got up and walked over to the stairs leading up to the playground next to the swings. She climbed up and after sliding down, turned to see Jeff watching her with his arms crossed.

"I saw you with him at the corn maze the other night."

"You were there? Why didn't you come up and say hi?" But of course, if she was with Will he couldn't have. "Sorry. I know you two try to avoid each other."

Jeff scoffed. "I try to avoid him. He seeks me out. I don't know where you were, but he came back later and threatened me. Told me to stay away from him, like somehow I'd followed him there. You can ask Lydia. She was with me."

So that was why Will had gone back in. He hadn't dropped something. He'd spotted Jeff.

She took a step forward and touched Jeff's arm. "Will lets grudges ruin his happiness. But you don't have to do that. Don't let him get to you."

Jeff frowned. "It's okay. Denny and I need to get back to L.A. soon anyway. And there are a lot fewer chances of running into him there."

She had mixed feelings about that news. He needed to get on with his life and staying here was holding him back from that.

"Well, don't be a stranger." She smiled and ducked her head. "Even if we're only friends."

***

The soothing swirl of cream in Will's coffee cup was in complete contrast to the situation at hand. Charlie had come home from work looking defeated. Usually, he was a ball of energy that never depleted, but not today. After dropping his car keys and jacket on the table, he'd sat down in a heap and ran his fingers through his hair, over and over, until his blond mane stuck up in every direction.

"What's with you?" Caroline nudged his jacket away from her with one finger and wiped the spot with a napkin.

"I don't want to tell Jane I'm leaving in a week. Every time I start to say it, I chicken out. I've got four days of work left. I have to be in San Francisco by Monday."

"Well, when she sees you packing up all your stuff, won't that make it kind of obvious?" Caroline smirked. "She dated you knowing you'd be leaving at some point. Why is this so hard?"

Will circled the rim of his cup with his finger. "The reason he can't tell her is because he hasn't decided how to leave things. Charlie, you owe her that. Don't make her be the one to ask."

Charlie nodded. "You're right." His hands continued to fidget, and he looked up at the ticking clock on the wall, a concentrated look on his face. "We've been together practically every free moment for over a month. What do I do now?"

Caroline leaned forward. "You need to make a clean break. Otherwise, you just prolong this thing."

"Or ..." Will glared at Caroline. "You could ask Jane to come visit you in San Francisco. I'll pay for the flight. You could choose not to date anyone new for a while and see if you two could make it work."

Caroline scoffed. "Not date someone new? Like that's gonna happen."

Charlie slouched onto the table top and rested his head on his arm. "Caroline's right. I hate being alone."

This was the side of Charlie that Will despised. The self-defeating, self-fulfilling cycle of doubting his own goodness.

Will stood up and ruffled Charlie's already messy hair. "Then I guess you know what you need to do." He went down the hall to get his laptop, but when he came back, Caroline was still harping on about what Charlie should say to Jane.

He swiped his coffee cup and set himself up in the den instead. Elsie was working tonight, and Jane was at home preparing to hand out candy to trick-or-treaters. Charlie would head over there later and probably pretend everything was fine. Knowing him, he'd wait until the very last moment to break her heart.

Numbers were easier to think about. Will got two minutes of work done before Charlie came in, wrestling with a bag of mini Snickers, which was about as loud as standing next to an avalanche. He finally got it open and set it down.

"If anyone rings the doorbell, will you hand these out? Caroline said she's heading to a nail appointment. She just broke one trying to open up a Diet Coke and found a place still open."

"Hmm." Whether or not Caroline was going to a nail appointment was not on his list of important information. He looked up from his computer and saw Charlie still standing there, looking dejected. But there was nothing more to say that would do any good. Will had already given his opinion.

"Are you gonna stick around here, Will? Since we're into November tomorrow, we'll have the whole month paid whether we want it or not."

Will gave Charlie a warning look. He didn't want to discuss it while Caroline was within hearing range, wanting to know why Will might or might not stay in Meryton. Unlike Charlie, he knew exactly what he would say to Elsie before he left, leaving nothing uncertain between them. And they weren't even a couple. It killed him that Charlie did this to girlfriends over and over again. Elsie was going to hate them both.

CHAPTER 15 ♥ SANDWICHES

The doorbell rang and the shipping box fortress Elsie had been building around her suddenly seemed like a mistake. She quickly gathered up the leftover Halloween candy wrappers and shoved them under the couch behind her.

"Coming!"

She moved aside a stack and weaved through the mess to reach the front door. The last thing she expected was to see Will Darcy on her doorstep.

"Jane said you were here getting orders ready to ship so I thought I'd join you. She and Charlie are watching the musical, *Cats*, at full volume and I can't get any work done."

Elsie wrinkled her nose. "Who would voluntarily watch that?"

"Right?"

She'd instinctively waved him in while he was talking, but was still not sure why he'd decided to come here. It wasn't like the library wasn't an option.

He didn't say anything about her cardboard towers, just carefully stepped through the path she'd made until he reached the couch. He pulled open his laptop and started flipping through a stack of paperwork he'd brought.

Apparently, he did just want a quiet place to work. She retrieved a stack of shipping bags off a chair and went back to folding T-shirts and inserting them in bags, before carefully affixing the sticky label to the front. They worked in companionable silence for a few minutes before he looked up.

"How's your business going?"

"It's fine." She thought about telling him they'd just gotten in a new shipment of T-shirts to press, but it still wouldn't explain why she liked to play with the boxes.

But there was something she and Jane had gone back and forth on and getting a third opinion wasn't a bad idea. "We'd like to offer free shipping from Black Friday until Christmas, but we can't agree on how to do it without raising T-shirt prices. We're afraid of a backlash from our customers."

Will looked thoughtful. "What are your margins now?"

"A pressed T-shirt costs us about three dollars and we sell them for 9.99."

"9.99 is a good price point. I don't think you can offer free shipping for one T-shirt, Elsie. No matter how much you raise the price. Shipping costs too much. Besides, you want to incentivize customers to spend more than they originally intended. Offer free shipping if they buy three or more shirts. That's what I'd do."

He went back to typing on his computer, and she went back to packing orders, lost in thought. He made it seem so simple. Jane had argued for free shipping when spending $50 or more, but counting T-shirts was much simpler on the customer, and most people didn't want five shirts. Good things came in threes.

"Good things come in threes."

"What?" Will looked up from his work.

"Good things come in threes. Would that make a good slogan? We could put it at the top of the website with the offer code."

"Sounds like a winner."

She jumped up and ran to her computer to make a graphic for it, excited to show Jane later. And then she checked recent orders and lost track of time for a while. Oh no. How long had she left Will alone in the living room? Ten minutes? An hour? Would he be upset?

She ran in to see him sitting in the same spot, working as if she'd never left.

"Sorry. Are you hungry?"

He glanced up. "Not unless you are."

She put her hands on her hips. "What kind of answer is that? Either you're hungry or you're not."

Will's brown eyes twinkled. "Haven't you ever been in between those two?"

"So you're kind of not hungry?"

"I could eat."

Now he was just teasing her. The man was exasperating.

He got up and walked to her, standing close. Too close. Her mouth went dry as his eyes gazed into hers. "I can see I'm making you huffy. Why don't we go get something to eat?"

"I'm not huffy," she whispered. His pinky finger brushed against hers and a shiver went through her. How could he go from staying off in his corner practically ignoring her, to this?

"Hangry then?"

"I've never been hangry."

He reached up and brushed a strand of her hair back from her face. Her heart was practically going to jump right out of her chest. This was a mistake. She didn't even like him. Charming men were dangerous. They easily hid their uglier side when it was convenient. And yet she couldn't pull her eyes away, even as his face moved a little closer.

Her cellphone jangled and danced on top of a box nearby, and Elsie lunged for it before it fell off. It was her mother, and normally she'd ignore it, but she'd been about to cross a line she swore she wouldn't cross. So she answered.

"Hi, Mom."

"Elsie, dear. You have to listen to me. Collin is packing up right this minute. He's stopped asking about you."

"That's a good thing, Mom." Elsie glanced at Will, hoping he wasn't hearing her mother's end of things. He didn't seem to be listening. He looked pensive, like his thoughts were elsewhere.

"It's worse. I checked his phone while he was in the bathroom. He's been texting back and forth with Charlotte Lucas for days. He called her 'his sweetie.' You have to do something, Elsie. All that money can't go to the Lucas's."

No way. There was no way Charlotte would be interested in Collin. "How do you know it's her? It could be anybody."

"Elsie Bennet, I'm not a fool. I looked up the number. It's her."

"Okay, well. Good luck to them. I gotta go." Elsie hung up before her mother could start begging again.

"Sorry about that. So, do you want to go somewhere or make something for dinner here?"

Will shrugged, no longer the teasing guy he'd been before. There was no reason to feel guilty about that. It was only a phone call. You were supposed to answer those.

"Follow me then. I make a mean roast beef sandwich."

***

Will wasn't just here for some peace and quiet. He was here to give Charlie a chance to talk to Jane. He'd made Charlie promise it would be tonight. There was no time left, and if Charlie put it off again, he'd probably end up sending Jane a text on his drive to the airport.

Was it selfish to take one last chance to win over Elsie while her sister got dumped? His conscience bothered him, there was no denying it. But he also liked being in her house. Elsie didn't hover, she didn't put on airs. She was just herself, hair in a messy bun, yoga pants, and a T-shirt that said, "Bookmarks are for quitters." When he wasn't completely exasperated with her, all he thought about was taking her in his arms and kissing her senseless.

At the moment, he was tending toward exasperated. The sandwich she'd made him was the driest thing he'd eaten in a long time, but she'd put the mayonnaise back in the fridge, and he didn't want to make a fuss when she already thought he was a food snob. He took a long drink of lemonade made from a powdered mix and wished he'd put in a vote to go out to a restaurant.

He looked up and saw Elsie eyeing him. "What's the matter, Will?"

"Nothing." He picked up his sandwich, putting on what he hoped was an enthusiastic face.

Elsie laughed. "Put the thing down. You are the worst actor I've ever seen. Worse than Lydia, and that's saying something. What's wrong with the sandwich? Do you not like roast beef?"

"I love roast beef. I could use a little more mayonnaise though. That's all."

She got up and got the jar out of the fridge. "That's because you didn't let me put mustard on it. You can't have roast beef without mustard."

"Says you."

"Says me." She took his plate from him and lathered a generous layer of mayonnaise on the bread.

Great, now it had too much. Why couldn't the woman let him make his own sandwich? It was time to be the real him. Holding back was exhausting. He picked up his knife and scraped half of it off. Then he put the sandwich back together and took a big bite. "Now it's perfect."

"You are fussy, Will Darcy. You know that, right?" Her exasperation only made him glad he did it.

"I can be exacting."

"I would have said trying."

"Fair enough. I like things a certain way."

"You like getting your way, Will." She was still teasing, but there was a bite to her tone that made him realize just how far he was from being in her good graces. And it had nothing to do with roast beef.

He stared her down and she ducked her head, blowing out a frustrated breath. "I'm sorry."

"I am too. I have high mayonnaise standards. They're impossible to live up to."

She gave him a small smile and they went back to eating. It was time to leave before she had to hint at it. He finished off the sandwich and rinsed his plate. "I'd better go."

She walked him to the door, probably eager to get rid of him.

***

After he left, Elsie threw herself into cleaning up the living room, putting away boxes and creating a pile that needed to be mailed. She'd take it all to the post office in the morning. How had they managed to start a fight over a sandwich? And why had she let herself turn it into something else? Her mouth got her in so much trouble sometimes.

She vacuumed the carpet, cleaned up the kitchen, and took a shower. Jane still wasn't home, and she wanted to talk to her about Will. Or any subject that would get her mind off him. Anything would be better than churning the situation around in her mind with no clear answer in sight.

Elsie eyed her phone. Was Charlotte really in a relationship with Collin? They'd been friends long enough that Elsie could ask, and Charlotte wouldn't lie. It was none of Elsie's business, except that someone had to tell Charlotte what a dumb idea it was. Who chased after someone because they had money?

Maybe she'd test the waters first with a text. Then Charlotte could ignore it or put it off if she wasn't ready to talk about it yet.

Are you dating Collin?

The little dots populating a response came and went several times. Finally, Charlotte texted back.

I'm sorry, Elsie. I should have told you.

Why are you sorry? I'm just curious.

I know things didn't work out between you two. I didn't mean to jump right in after.

Elsie started to type out a response and then immediately erased it. Charlotte actually thought she'd be jealous? What was there to be jealous of?

Don't take this the wrong way, Char. Is this about his money?

He's a good guy and he likes me. Mostly I just want to get out of this town. Collin's using his connections to get me a job at a nice salon in L.A. and an apartment of my own. I'm 26. I don't want to live with my parents forever.

So she'll live off a rich guy. But Elsie couldn't say that. Charlotte was honest to a fault. And practical. So practical she never worried about intangible things like love. She wouldn't spend all his money, but she wouldn't turn it down either. If Collin was this desperate to be in a relationship, then Charlotte was doing him a service, because the next gal he propositioned after one date would bleed him dry.

She couldn't wait to tell Jane, though she knew her sister would naively wish the couple happiness and true love. That seemed about as likely as an alien invasion. And right then, a jingle of keys sounded outside the front door. Elsie jumped up. In her stocking feet, she slid across the tile floor in one move and leaped to the carpet. Too bad no one was around to appreciate her secret talent.

"Jane!" Elsie flipped the lock and opened the door for her sister. "You'll never guess—"

Jane looked up from her keys with red-rimmed eyes.

"What's the matter?"

Jane burst into tears and rushed past her, grabbing the box of tissues they always kept on a table in the living room. She blew her nose loudly and sank to the floor, putting her back against the couch.

"I'm so dumb."

"No, you're not." Elsie went over and sat next to her. Jane was still crying too much to explain more, so Elsie waited, calculating out how long Charlie had been in Meryton. Very few things upset Jane like this, and Elsie realized just how far Jane must have fallen for him.

"Charlie's leaving?" Elsie finally asked.

Jane nodded and wiped her nose on her sleeve, despite the handful of tissues she was clutching. "He said it's been fun and he's so glad he got to know me. Oh, Elsie. I feel like the biggest fool."

"He's the biggest fool."

Jane shook her head. "Don't say that." As hurt as she was, she was still defending him.

"So, that's it?"

"Yep."

"I can't believe it. He was really that casual about it?"

Jane shrugged one shoulder. "He did look pretty miserable, but I swear that's what came out of his mouth. He leaves tomorrow."

Elsie stood up and paced. He'd put off telling Jane until the last minute. She wasn't sure if it was sweet or extremely rude. "Where does he go next?"

"San Francisco."

"Aunt Diane and Uncle Steve are in San Francisco. They'd love for you to visit."

"Elsie, don't. He made it pretty clear we're done." Jane stood up and headed into the kitchen. "All I want right now is a cup of tea and some mindless television."

Elsie went around her and put on the tea kettle. She didn't talk about Charlotte and Collin, or Will coming over. None of that seemed particularly important when her sister was hurting.

CHAPTER 16 ♥ "HOW IS JANE DOING?"

Most mornings, Elsie shuffled into the kitchen to find Jane fully dressed, eating breakfast while watching one of the perky network morning shows. But today the kitchen was dark and silent.

Elsie went to check on her, but didn't have the heart to wake her up once she saw Jane curled up against her pillow with a comforter pulled up to her nose.

She hadn't said when Charlie was leaving today. Perhaps there was still time.

Elsie had a bad habit of meddling. She couldn't help it when so many people around her made stupid decisions all the time. She debated whether to walk down and have a talk with Charlie herself. If things were really over, as Jane insisted they were, it would make little difference whether Elsie made a fool of herself on Jane's behalf. Jane wouldn't have to know.

She loaded up her car with the prepared shipping packages and drove down the street, parking in front of Charlie and Will's house. Charlie's car was still parked in the driveway. Will's was not. Perfect.

She went to the front door, fighting the feeling she should head to the post office and mind her own business. That feeling went into overdrive when Caroline answered.

"Yes?" Caroline asked, as if Elsie were some random salesperson knocking at the door.

"Has Charlie left yet?"

Caroline sighed. "Not yet. But we're leaving as soon as he and

Will get back from running errands, so if you have a message for him, can you just give it to me? I want to get back to L.A. before this afternoon's rush hour traffic hits."

There was no message worth transporting through Caroline. Every look she gave Elsie demonstrated a strong dislike, though Elsie wasn't sure what she'd done to deserve it.

"Never mind. I was heading to the post office and thought I'd stop and say goodbye."

Caroline gave her a syrupy, pseudo-sympathetic smile. "How is Jane doing?"

Elsie tensed. "She's fine."

"Well good. Charlie was worried about what to do, but after talking it over with me and Will, he knew it was best to make a clean break of things." Caroline leaned against the doorframe, hiding half a smile. She wanted the news to bother Elsie. And it did.

Elsie's ears grew hot and her throat closed off. She knew she needed to turn around and walk off before she said something she'd regret. And everything running through her head at the moment was not something she wanted to say aloud. Why was Charlie so easily influenced?

"Okay, bye." Elsie ran down the walk and got into her car. Caroline was a terrible person. Will was a terrible person. She knew that. So why did it hurt so much to know what Will had done?

***

Will did all the responsible things. He checked the oil and tire pressure, carried Caroline's two enormous suitcases out for her, gathered up phone chargers, and packed up any leftover food Charlie wanted to take with him. That's what their last conversation had been about. Cleaning out the fridge.

Charlie had to be regretting his decision, but he stubbornly moved ahead as if he was fine with it. Will was not stupid. He'd seen the last forlorn look Charlie gave to Jane's house. But he'd driven away anyway.

And now Will was sitting in an empty rental house in a neighborhood that surely hated him. He rubbed his forehead and forced himself away from the front window.

Whether he was staying three more days or three more weeks, it was best to get ahead on preparations. He vacuumed out Charlie and Caroline's bare rooms, threw out a soap end left in their shower, and took out the liner in their bathroom trash.

Then he ate dinner in front of the TV and tried not to think about Elsie. Tomorrow was the day she and her father usually went to the library.

It would do no good to hide out in this house, and he doubted she would appreciate him showing up on her doorstep again. He'd make sure to run into her at the library and lay it all out. Then he could leave Meryton with no regrets.

CHAPTER 17 ♥ "THIS IS YOUR OPINION OF ME?"

"I'm okay, Elsie. You can quit hovering."

"I'm not hovering." Okay, she was totally hovering, but Elsie didn't know what else to do. She couldn't make it hurt less for Jane, but she wanted to anyway. So she'd made breakfast and sat next to Jane, pouring her orange juice for her and grabbing a napkin when Jane dropped a bit of egg on the table.

"You can go with Dad to the library. I'll be fine here. I gave the whole thing a lot of thought last night and think I overreacted. Charlie never made any promises to me. He's moving on. I need to as well."

Elsie glared at her sister. "Jane. There is no shame in not being ready to move on right away. I don't think you misread the situation. He did. And Will and Caroline were eager to encourage him to get out of here. I'm not convinced they didn't coerce him into breaking up with you."

Jane shook her head. "Charlie is a grown man. He makes his own choices." She stared down at her plate. "He just decided not to choose me."

"I hate people." Elsie picked up her own plate and scraped her bread crusts into the garbage can. "You deserve better, Jane. But I'm starting to think there's no one out there that has any sense left. Did you know Charlotte is dating Collin? She's letting him pay for her to have an apartment in L.A."

Jane's eyes went wide. "Wow. They must have really fallen for each other."

"Um. No. But I have no doubt Charlotte will make the best of it. She's nothing if not resourceful."

"Elsie." Jane's eyes shown with disapproval. "This is your best friend you're talking about."

"I know. That's why I can say it and still have love for her in my heart." Elsie rinsed her plate and turned to leave the kitchen. "Are you sure you'll be okay here?"

Jane waved her off and reached over, turning up the volume on the TV. An energetic newscaster was demonstrating a stain removal product. Can't-miss stuff right there.

Elsie got in her car and drove down the street, parking in her parents' driveway. She glanced over at Charlie and Will's house with no cars in front. Hopefully whoever rented it next would cause less drama in the neighborhood.

Her dad was ready for her when she went inside, but they weren't quick enough to avoid Mrs. Bennet, who stalked around the corner, her hair curlers shaking as she raised a finger to Elsie.

"You stop right there and speak to your mother before you go running off. Collin paid you special attention and you acted as if it was nothing!"

"I don't like him. Why should I pretend? For money?" Elsie stared her down, daring her to admit what this was really about.

Her dad put a steadying hand on Elsie's arm and turned to his wife. "Leave it be, dear. Would you want Elsie running off to L.A. with him anyway? Life is good. Enjoy your morning. We're heading off to the library."

Mrs. Bennet huffed and turned to head back in the kitchen. She'd continue to hold a grudge, but at least they were on their way.

Elsie drove to the back end of the library parking lot and helped her dad out of the car. When they'd almost reached the entrance, she noticed a black sedan that looked an awful lot like Will's. She forced her shoulders to relax. It was her mind playing tricks on her. Will was gone, and her subconscious was bringing up things to remind her of him.

They said hello to Mrs. Lucas at the front desk before finding their usual table in the back. Her dad went to browse through a row of books and Elsie cracked open hers, though her mind was already elsewhere, wondering if Mrs. Lucas knew Charlotte was leaving and how she felt about it.

"Elsie."

Elsie glanced behind her and sucked in a quick breath. Will was half tucked behind a bookshelf, watching her. He beckoned with a finger and Elsie stood, checking to see that her dad was still preoccupied. What was Will doing here? Maybe it had something to do with Jane and Charlie.

When she drew closer, Will reached out and took her hand, leading her deeper into the row. He kept her hand even when they stopped.

"I always say the wrong thing around you and I have no doubt I'll mess it up now. Forgive me."

Elsie instinctively pulled her hand away. Will always left her so conflicted. She hated him and yet wanted to be near him. It couldn't be healthy.

"What are you doing here, Will? I—"

He closed the distance between them, his hand cupping the back of her neck, and he kissed her with a soft fierceness that temporarily froze her in place. Her lips slid against his, and she sighed as his thumb caressed the line of her jaw. She'd always longed to be kissed like this. As if everything else in the world was a fuzzy second to this moment in time. And then logic took hold and she placed both hands against his chest and pushed him back.

He put his hands up in surrender. "I'm sorry. I shouldn't have done that. It's just, I didn't want to leave without asking how you felt about us. If you would ever consider getting to know me. The real me. Because the truth is, I really, really like you, Elsie. And I'm willing to stay here for as long as it takes for you to decide."

"I don't need time to decide." She took a step back, afraid he might kiss her again and terrified of the part of her that wanted him to. "After what you did to Jane and Charlie, and to Jeff and your sister, there's no way I could see us together. You control people, Will. I don't want to be controlled."

His eyes narrowed. "This is your opinion of me?"

"Yes." She swallowed back the unease she felt in saying it after he'd just declared his feelings. But it was for the best. Someone needed to wake him up. "You didn't go back for a watch the other night. You went back to bother Jeff. He hadn't even come near us. He can't even be in the same town with you."

His shook his head. "Stop, just stop." He swallowed hard and his eyes seemed to pierce right through her. "I won't bother you again. Bye, Elsie."

He turned and left. She heard the loud clunk of him pressing down on the door lever and the solid finality of the door shutting behind him. She sank down and hugged her knees. Why she was crying, she wasn't sure, but her quiet tears helped relieve the tightly wound feelings demanding to be let out.

Her dad found her several minutes later, and she scrambled to her feet before he could bend down to try to help her up.

"Oh, Dad." She hugged him, and he patted her back.

"I don't know what's wrong, dear, but you don't cry very often so it must be something serious. Do you want to talk about it?"

She shook her head into his shoulder.

"You ready to go? I have plenty of books to last me the week."

She nodded and wiped her face, trying to make herself presentable before having to go up to the checkout counter.

They walked out slowly together, and her dad didn't ask a thing about it. He gave her one more hug as she brought him to the door of his house and he turned and smiled. "Don't come in. Go see Jane. She'll be a lot more helpful than your mother if she sees you like this."

Elsie nodded and ran back to her car. She wasn't sure she was up to telling even Jane, but Jane met her at the door, holding a folded slip of notebook paper secured with tape.

"Will dropped this off for you. I'm heading to the post office, but I want to hear all about this mystery note when I get back."

CHAPTER 18 ♥ SINCERELY, WILL DARCY

The letter ripped a little as she tried to unseal the tape and Elsie considered tearing the whole thing up, but she owed it to Will to read it, and in all honesty, she was dying to know what it might say.

Dear Elsie,

Don't worry. I'm leaving town immediately and you won't have to see me again. But I hate that you've been duped by Jeff, and worse, that he seems to have turned it into a game. So, though I don't want to dredge it all back up, I feel I have to.

You are correct. I didn't go back into the corn maze for a watch. I went back for Jeff. I spotted him making out with your sister, Lydia, and I went to go talk to them. Yes, it was a pointless, meddling thing to do, but I was under the impression you had feelings for him, and also, I was worried about Lydia being with someone so much older and more experienced. She assured me it was none of my business.

I'm assuming Jeff mentioned seeing me there. Though why, I can only guess. He has a history of toying with people, including my sister, Gianna. She was only fourteen when our mother died and took it very hard. She started sneaking into our family's liquor cabinet and it was a while before my father figured it out. I left college for a semester and came back to help. She went to therapy, and we removed all alcohol from the house. It was our family secret. My dad was huge on appearances and no one could know about it. Unfortunately, she confided in Jeff.

Jeff and I had been childhood friends until things started disappearing from our house after his visits. He was intimidating and manipulative, even back then, and when he blamed me for some missing money, I let him. But I also told him I didn't want to be friends anymore. I didn't see much of him until after my dad died. Jeff suddenly took an interest in Gianna. She was eighteen and I was busy, trying to get my business off the ground and handle the inheritance. He tempted her with alcohol and promises that he cared about her, that I didn't, and that she deserved her portion of the inheritance immediately.

The night of the accident, I called her, wanting to know where she was. She wouldn't talk to me. She handed the phone to Jeff, who told me they were fine and not to worry. Right before he hung up, I heard the crash, and the screams, and then the call ended.

I will always wonder if the accident was partially my fault. After all, he'd run a red light and plowed straight into a large truck while on the phone with me. But he was drunk and he knew it. He squeezed out of the crumpled car and tried to make a run for it, leaving Gianna trapped and badly injured. Witnesses tracked him down and held onto him until the police arrived. Gianna was taken to the hospital where she underwent surgery. It didn't matter. She is paralyzed from the waist down and always will be.

If keeping him away from her makes me controlling, then so be it. She's all I have left. Secret keeping is in my blood, but I can see now it's time to let that go.

Sincerely,
Will Darcy

P.S. I had high hopes for Jane and Charlie. He was afraid a long distance relationship wouldn't work, as it's been a disaster for him in the past. The only thing I urged him to do was let Jane know.

Elsie dropped the letter and plopped onto the couch. It was too much to take. Her mind went to a million places. Jane reduced to a P.S.? Gianna paralyzed? Jeff had never once mentioned that when he talked about the accident. He'd only mentioned the consequences for him. She got up and ran to her laptop, typing Gianna Darcy into a Google search. The top result: Gianna's wheelchair basketball team raising money for charity.

Of course. Why would Will lie about his own sister? Why had Elsie been so quick to take Jeff at his word? She hadn't jumped up to do a Google search then. She'd been so blind. So very blind and foolish. Yes, Will was a grump and he'd been rude to her when they'd met. Her pride had been hurt and everything he'd said and done after had been tainted by her early opinion of him.

She'd always prided herself on being logical and fair. She'd been neither.

***

Will packed up quickly, trying to tamp down his churning thoughts so he could focus on the task at hand. The last thing he needed was a trip back here because he'd left something important. But he couldn't stop reliving the way Elsie had clung to him for a moment, as caught up in their kiss as he was. Stubborn girl, she wouldn't let go of that grudge she held against him. All the while accusing him of holding grudges. Jeff had poisoned her, but it wouldn't have worked if Will had acted friendly from the very beginning. Yes, Elsie was stubborn, but he was a fool and he'd ruined this.

It had been a long time since someone had captured his attention so fully. But he'd have to let it go. It wasn't meant to be.

He went around the rental house one more time, systematically turning off lights and checking locks. After dropping the key off with the owner, he drove straight to L.A., only stopping for gas. He almost hoped Gianna wouldn't be home, but she greeted him the moment he came inside.

"Why didn't you tell me you were coming?" She looked down at his suitcase and then up at his frown. "What happened?"

"Charlie's moved on to San Francisco. I think I'll stay here for a while. That should make you happy."

"Seeing you always makes me happy." She eyed him curiously

but didn't press further. "Are you hungry?"

"Starving." He hadn't eaten since breakfast that morning.

"Great. I'll make you an omelet."

Gianna wheeled into the kitchen and immediately started browsing in the fridge, using her long grabber. He'd wanted to buy her a refrigerator that went under the counter, but she wouldn't hear of it, preferring her shiny stainless steel beauty.

"What can I do to help?"

She handed him a bag of green onions. "Chop these up fine."

He got to work and soon the kitchen smelled wonderful. Like browning butter and fresh herbs. He flipped on her iPod, sitting in its docking station. Their mother had always listened to Otis Redding while puttering away in the kitchen, and they liked to carry on the tradition.

He got lost in "These Arms of Mine," reveling in the depression music like that evoked. But it could only be today. Starting tomorrow he wouldn't think about Elsie again.

"You want to talk about her?" Gianna asked, a small smile slipping as she caught him lost in thought.

He sighed. "Not really." He couldn't tell her about Jeff's involvement. After the accident, Gianna had thrown herself into her recovery. She rarely spoke of Jeff and always with pain. Jeff had actually tried to claim she was the one driving and they'd swapped seats right after the accident. It made no logical sense, considering the fire department had to use the Jaws of Life to get her out. But then, nothing about Jeff Wickham made logical sense.

"What happened with Charlie and Jane?"

"What do you think?"

Gianna cocked her head. "Again? I think the phrase 'string of broken hearts' was named after that rascal."

"And yet he's such a nice guy." Will's best friend was an unexpected personality paradox.

"Do you think it's because the Bingley's are so..." Gianna motioned with her spatula, trying to come up with the right word.

Will smiled. "Distant? Demanding? You could fill in that sentence with so many things, Gianna. And yes. I do think that's why Charlie can't commit to anyone. His parents probably haven't touched each other in twenty years. That's commitment right there. A rock-solid relationship."

"Oh, Will. You're terrible." She laughed, shaking her head at him. "But I'm glad you're home."

***

Elsie hid in the office, trying to draw new T-shirt designs, but everything turned out terrible. She finally pulled out the letter from Will and read it through again. Then she slid the thing in the paper cutter and sliced off the P.S. at the bottom before stalking down the hall to Jane's room.

Compartmentalizing their individual suffering was not helping, but she would at least spare her sister Will's callous explanation of Charlie's decision.

"Will came to see me at the library today."

Jane's eyes widened. "What did he say?"

"He said ..." His words came back to Elsie and it hurt to think of what she'd said in return, about him being controlling. No one likes to admit they've been a complete idiot, even to their sister. "He said he really, really liked me and he wanted to stay and see if..." Elsie sat down on the floor and picked at the rug. "It doesn't matter because I shut him down. I told him he was controlling and I asked him about going back for the watch he supposedly dropped. There was no watch. He went to confront Jeff."

"Will wanted to stay for you?" Jane put a hand to her forehead. "Wow. Oh wow." But she must have realized her excitement was making Elsie feel worse. "Confront Jeff about what?"

Elsie pulled out the letter and let it flutter down onto the bed next to Jane. "This will explain better. I'm going to go get some hot chocolate. You want some?"

Jane waved her off, already too immersed in the letter to answer. Elsie took that as a yes and went to the kitchen to prepare two mugs.

It was several minutes before she got returned to Jane's room, but Jane was still busy reading, or more likely, rereading. Elsie handed her a mug and carefully sat back down with her own.

Jane looked up. "This explains Will's weird questions about Lydia. That girl. You have to go talk to her."

Elsie's shoulders slumped. "I know. But maybe you should. She likes you better."

Jane took a sip. "Maybe so, but she doesn't listen to me any better than she listens to you."

117

"I could approach Jeff first. He said he was heading back to L.A. I hope he is."

Jane's eyes lit up. "That might be better. Maybe he'll come clean about the whole thing and apologize."

"Jane. Did you even read the letter? He put Will's sister in a wheelchair. He's a manipulative monster. I don't see this going well no matter how I approach it."

Elsie took out her phone, reminding herself that Jeff didn't know about any of this and it would be normal for her to text him.

Hey. Have you left for LA yet?

Not yet. Denny says he's not ready. He met someone, lucky dog.

Likely story. Elsie was too mad to answer and put down her phone. "He's not leaving."

"You could tell Mom and Dad."

They rarely interfered in Lydia's life these days, but this was a whole different level of trouble. "Yes, I think you're right, Jane. I'll talk to Dad, and then I'll talk to Lydia." Elsie stood and retrieved the letter from the bed, carefully folding it back up.

"You're not going right now are you?" Jane asked.

Elsie nodded. "Actually, I think I am."

CHAPTER 19 ♥ SUSPICION

"Dad, you're not listening. Lydia still lives at home. Can't you ground her or something? Cut off her phone like you did before?"

Elsie's dad wrinkled his nose. "I thought you liked Jeff? Did he break up with you? Is that why you were crying in the library this morning? I'm sorry, Elsie. Him choosing Lydia over you is terrible, but not a reason to take away her phone."

"Dad, I don't care about Jeff. Not romantically, anyway. And now that I've learned some things about his past I can't even be friends with him. He will be a toxic influence on Lydia. Can't you just trust me on that? How am I going to convince Lydia of it if you don't believe me?"

"I believe in your character judgment. If you say Jeff is a bad guy then I believe you. But Lydia goes through boyfriends like toilet paper. Why make all this fuss about this one or that one? I can already hear the screaming. It's not worth it."

Elsie rubbed her head. Lately, peace and quiet were all he cared about. "Has Jeff been over here recently?"

He shrugged. "He's here all the time. Your mother loves him."

"I'm sure she does. Where is Lydia, anyway?"

"No idea. Look, I'll send her over when she shows up. Then you and Jane can sit her down and have your chat."

There was little else she could do. But she didn't need to wait for him to pass on the message. She pulled out her phone and texted Lydia on the walk back to her house.

Where R U?

She reached her door before Lydia bothered to respond.

At home. Why?

Elsie glanced back. Sure enough, Lydia was pulling in her parents' driveway. Elsie jogged back and reached Lydia before she could head into the house.

"What has you so worked up?" Lydia asked, looking amused.

"Nothing. I mean, I'm not worked up. Are you dating Jeff?" Lydia hemmed, before finally admitting. "Yeah, I guess."

"He tried to kiss me last week. Strange he would wait until he was already dating you."

Lydia glared. "What are you saying? That Jeff's cheating on me? Because he'd already told me all about the two of you. We don't keep secrets from each other."

Elsie had taken the wrong approach, though maybe there was no right one. "Lydia. I'm not mad at you. I don't care that you're dating Jeff except that I've found out some things about him that worry me."

"Let me guess. Will Darcy talked to you? It's all made up. It's all lies, Elsie." Her eyes widened. "Wait. Will told you about seeing us at the corn maze, didn't he? He promised he wouldn't say anything."

"I don't know what Will promised or didn't promise you. All I know is that his sister is paralyzed because of Jeff. He caused a car accident and then just left her there. And it doesn't seem like Jeff cares all that much about it. I don't think he cares much about anything. I just wanted to warn you, from one sister to another. That's all." Elsie backed up and turned to go. She'd done her best, and there wasn't more she could do.

"Okay, whatever," Lydia called after her.

***

It was nice to get back to a routine. Will and Gianna played basketball almost every morning, and then he worked in the den, making phone calls and catching up on invoices. He had his favorite desk chair with amazing lumbar support and the buttery feel of plush leather. There were no interruptions from Charlie or attempts to drag him anywhere.

Except for one quick trip to Phoenix mid-week to meet with contractors, he was free to be alone until dinner, when Gianna would cook his favorite foods. He was content, and just because he had to keep reminding himself how content he was, it did not negate the truth of it. Whenever Elsie came to mind he firmly pushed her back out. It had been two weeks. In no time at all, he wouldn't even remember her. He imagined she felt the same way about him.

All caught up on work, he focused his attention back on the Darcy Foundation. It irked him that his parents had to put the family name on it. So much of their personal lives had been a secret, except of course letting the world know how philanthropic they were. He'd change it now, only Gianna insisted their family name was the reason many of their generous donors still gave to it. He hated that she was right. Especially since he refused to host galas or hold fancy auctions in order to find new ones.

What he cared about most was making sure the money, every cent of it, went to good use. His parents had built a solid foundation, but he and Gianna had decided to change the focus. Researching spinal injuries was of course a priority, but Will's baby was opening a tuition-free trade school with flexible hours for working families. The trades were carefully chosen to maximize the student's future income and help build a lasting career. Championing things like welding, plumbing, and auto mechanics might not have been something his parents had ever considered, but Will knew they were needed jobs that would pull people way beyond minimum wage. They'd added onsite childcare and were working on branching out to several new locations. His latest challenge was getting local businesses on board, ready to hire the graduates.

He got back from a successful lunch meeting with the owner of a plumbing company and went inside to tell Gianna the good news. Gianna was playing basketball in the former ballroom with her physical therapist, Becky.

"Hello, Will." Becky passed him the ball, her thrust so strong it felt like catching a freight train. When he'd called her Brumhilda, he'd only been half-joking. She was one of the most intimidating people he'd ever met, both in presence and in her ability to get her own way. Any physical therapy argument with her quickly ended when she started in on constipation or a blood pressure diatribe until he or Gianna wished they'd never opened their mouths to begin with.

"How did the meeting with the plumbing company go?" Gianna asked.

"Good. They're hoping to hire ten more people this year and they promised to consider our graduates first."

Becky motioned for him to pass the ball back, clearly impatient to get Gianna moving again. He wasn't dressed for basketball, nor was he all that interested in Becky's elbow jabs, her favorite defensive strategy. He passed back the ball and headed toward the exit.

"You should call Charlie," Gianna called after him.

He poked his head back in. "Why? Did he call?"

Gianna shook her head. "Just a feeling I have. Besides, with Thanksgiving on Thursday, he's probably homesick. Are you sure he can't fly down for one day?"

Gianna and her big heart. She was always thinking about someone. He pulled out his cell when he reached the den and dialed Charlie's number. It had been a while since he'd heard from him.

Charlie answered right away. "Hey, Will. Back in L.A.?"

"Yeah. How's San Francisco?"

"It's great. I love it. It's beautiful here." Charlie's voice sounded overly cheerful, even for him, like he was fighting to make it sound believable.

"Is Caroline with you?"

"Nah. She came for a little sightseeing and left. Mom and Dad want at least one kid home for Thanksgiving."

"So you're staying there? You're always welcome here, you know I'd pay to fly you in and out."

Charlie sighed. "Nah. There are all sorts of problems with the project and they're paying me triple to stay and work. Oh, and the company put me up with an older couple who will feed me all the turkey and mashed potatoes I could possibly eat. They have an apartment on their property and they baby me like I'm their own son. I had chocolate chip pancakes this morning with Mickey Mouse ears. She packed me a lunch too. Egg salad sandwiches. I haven't eaten egg salad in years. Now I remember why. But it was a nice gesture, all the same."

It sounded like Charlie was getting all the pampering he craved. "So, how long should you be there?"

"A few more weeks and then it's back to L.A. They might

actually keep me at a desk for a while. Imagine that."

"I can't imagine you sitting in one place for more than five minutes."

"Me either. I'm thinking I'll trade out my chair for one of those exercise balls. That should help."

There was a long pause, while Will debated whether to bring up Meryton, or Jane, or worst of all, whether Charlie had met anyone new. He wasn't one to sit at home, nice older couple to chat with or not.

"Did you leave Meryton right away?" Charlie finally asked.

"Yeah," Will lied. "Right after you."

"Thanks for taking care of things. The homeowner already sent back the deposit we put down."

"Good. Good."

Charlie sighed. "Will. You can say it. You're disappointed in me. It's okay. I'm disappointed in myself. But what's done is done."

"Is it? You could call her." Dang. He was back to doling out unwanted advice. "Never mind. I shouldn't have said that."

Charlie was quiet for a few seconds. "It's fine. I gotta go, though. My crew is waiting on me."

"Of course. See you later." Will hung up and opened his laptop. He needed something else to think about. Something that wouldn't remind him of what they'd both left behind in Meryton.

***

Being on non-speaking terms with Lydia was not much different than their normal relationship, but Elsie still felt bad about their conversation and the deeper chasm it put between them. She even gathered up the clothes she'd confiscated from Lydia's shopping spree, though she hadn't been paid back for them, and brought the lot over as a peace offering. Two months in storage was punishment enough.

There was an ulterior motive to getting back into Lydia's good graces. Elsie wanted to know what was going on with Jeff. He'd stopped texting and the one time she saw him in town, he was friendly, but aloof, and quickly made excuses to leave. Lydia had obviously tipped him off.

He hadn't been seen at the house much either, according to her dad. Rather than letting her guard down, Elsie was feeling even more paranoid about it.

More Google searches revealed details about the crash. About the unnamed hit-and-run driver held down by witnesses, about Gianna's slow recovery. She'd also found an interesting You-Tube video, where Jeff and Denny posed as day-trading experts for a company called *Quit Your Day Job!* For ten-thousand dollars, you too could learn how to make millions during a bear market. How Jeff had become affiliated with the get-rich-quick scam was anyone's guess.

It made so much more sense. There was a lot more money to be made by recruiting people into day trading than actually being successful at something like that.

Lydia sent a thank you text, acknowledging the return of all her shopping bags, but when Elsie pressed into her whereabouts, Lydia stopped texting back.

"Of course." Elsie tossed down her phone after giving up on getting an answer and went to go change for work. She rotated through three pairs of grease-stained jeans. Under her work apron, it didn't matter what she wore. Especially now that her social life had completely dried up. If only she hadn't decided to side with a criminal.

Would Will really have stuck around for her? Would she have wanted him to? He hated Meryton. The memory of their argument in the library filled her with dread and longing at the same time.

"Elsie, where are you?" Jane came down the hall and found Elsie wrestling into her jeans.

"I swear these fit a week ago. Darn Thanksgiving pies. We have to start working out again, okay?"

Jane nodded. "We should probably stop drinking hot chocolate every night too."

Elsie wasn't quite as ready to commit to that. "Where have you been?"

Jane sighed. "At Mom and Dad's. Lydia's gone off to another audition in L.A., but she didn't take Kat this time and Kat's feelings are hurt."

Elsie stood up, sucking in to button her pants. "Lydia doesn't go alone anywhere. You know what this means, don't you?"

Jane raised an eyebrow. "Elsie, I think you need to let the whole Jeff thing go. Lydia's not a drinker. You know as well as I do she violently pukes if she has much of anything. What are you worried is going to happen?"

Elsie picked up her purse from the bed and put the strap on her shoulder. "I don't know. That's the problem. I don't know."

CHAPTER 20 ♥ BAD GUY

Will woke in the night knowing something was wrong, but still too disoriented to know what had created the feeling. His ears and eyes took a few seconds to begin working again and then he heard it. A soft giggle and a scraping noise outside.

He threw off the covers and peeked through the blinds, though he knew the view outside would be completely blocked by the laurel tree in front of his window. And now he heard nothing, though his whole body tensed, just waiting for something to happen. He knew he hadn't imagined it.

They'd had outside cameras installed after an attempted break-in years ago, and he threw on a robe and went to the kitchen, checked the camera images one by one, especially the camera trained on where he'd parked his car. No strange intruders lurked in any of them, and his car alarm hadn't gone off.

He stalked out of the kitchen, grabbing a poker from the fireplace on his way to the front door. Cautiously, he eked the door open and listened. Nothing.

He took a step outside and his foot smeared into something soft and gooey. And oh, that smell. Of all the awful, low-down, things to do. He'd fallen for a trick teenagers hadn't tired of in several generations. At least it wasn't in a flaming bag, though that was no comfort for his poor foot. What to do now? The last thing he wanted was to bring the stuff inside, but he wasn't about to venture out to the hose to find heaven knows what else waiting for him. They'd better not touch his car. He should have put it in the garage long ago. If they'd sold Dad's Bentley, like they'd been talking about for months, nothing would be sitting out in the open.

He firmly shut and locked the front door and hopped back to the nearest bathroom. Taking the liner out of the trash can, he used it to scrape the mess off his foot. "Stinking dog poop," he muttered as he grabbed a roll of paper towels from under the sink. He wet a few, doused them with liquid hand soap, and washed it off as best he could before tying the paper towels up in the bag in a tight knot. Then he turned on the shower water and scrubbed his feet and hands.

If it was just the poop he wouldn't bother calling the police. They'd only laugh at him and offer their sympathies. What was a disgusting, yet harmless, trick when there were murderers and thieves to track down? But he wouldn't be able to sleep until he knew if that was all they'd done.

He turned on the front lights and headed out with a heavy flashlight, constantly checking his surroundings to make sure no one could sneak up on him. At almost five in the morning, it was awfully dark out. He went immediately to his car and his stomach dropped. Four slashed tires and spray paint down one side, spelling out an obscenity. This, with the gift at the front door, felt very personal, and there was only one person he could think of who would stoop to such a level to let him know how he felt.

Will immediately reported it to the police. While he waited for them to send an officer, he took pictures and then went inside to check the cameras again, this time, going back far enough to see the surveillance a half hour before he'd awoken.

They were quick. The two people only took ten, maybe fifteen seconds by the car. Then one of them ran to the front door to deliver the poop. Both wore large hoodies, though it didn't hide the fact that the smaller one was most definitely a woman.

***

The flowers in the decorative pot by their front door were drooping and Elsie dropped the mail on the welcome mat so she could get the hose. Jane usually took care of them, but despite all her claims to being over Charlie, she wasn't quite the same. There were several times when Elsie spoke to her and she didn't hear until Elsie repeated herself. Jane's mind was just … elsewhere.

For the hundredth time, Elsie wished she could help, but for now, taking care of things Jane used to care about was all she could think to do.

The kid that usually mowed their lawn had broken his leg attempting a trampoline trick and the grass was reaching unkempt yard status. Elsie sighed. She could use the exercise anyway. She pulled their push mower out of the garage and attached the extension cord, plugging it in near the front door.

She ran in to grab her earbuds and soon was making satisfying headway across the front grass to the sounds of The Beatles.

She growled when *Let It Be* was interrupted by an incoming phone call and paused the mower, wiping her hands on her jeans before answering.

"Everything okay, Mom?"

"No, everything is not okay. Come right now. It's Lydia. She's been arrested."

"What? I'll be right over." Elsie hung up and immediately pulled the extension cord out of the mower, wrapping it in quick circles from elbow to palm until she reached where it was plugged in and yanked it out of the wall. She dropped the cord at the doorstep, opened the door, and threw the mail inside. Then she ran to her parent's house, hoping this was all blown out of proportion but fearing the worst. To her mind, there was nothing worse than misguided optimism.

"Elsie!" her mother threw open the door and wrapped her arms around her daughter in an unusual display of physical affection.

"Tell me what's going on. Where's Dad?"

"I'm right here." Dad sat on the couch looking defeated. "Jane is on her way. She was running an errand for me. Kat, get in here."

Kat slinked around the corner and sat meekly next to her Dad. "I didn't know about any of this, I swear."

"But you knew Lydia was with Jeff?"

"Didn't you? It was kind of obvious." Kat glared at the floor. "If I'd been with her she never would have done something like this."

"Well don't worry. Rules are changing around here. For one, you need to get a job and start acting responsibly if you want to continue living here. Look at Elsie. She has two jobs."

"Will someone please tell me what happened?" Elsie cut in, exasperated. Although she agreed about Kat getting a job.

Dad looked up. "I'm sorry I didn't listen to you earlier, Elsie. Apparently, Lydia and Jeff vandalized Will Darcy's car."

Elsie dropped to the couch and gripped her head in her hands. "No. Please no." She felt guilty by association. Guilty for enabling Jeff's victimhood, for buying his stories. "Vandalized how?"

Dad shook his head. "I'm not sure. All Lydia said was the police pulled them over for speeding through his neighborhood, and when they saw the can of spray paint in the back seat of her car and the smell and residue of it on Jeff's hands, they detained them. I'm sure once Will Darcy reported the damage they put it all together."

Elsie wished she had somewhere to crawl and hide from this. What must Will think of her family now?

Kat tapped on her phone. "You didn't mention the smell of marijuana in the car. So, I've been Googling vandalism. It's going to be a felony for sure. It says here if it's over $400 in damage and maliciously done, she's screwed."

"We'll have to get her a lawyer," their mother screeched, pacing around the room. "We have to post bail and get her out of there right now. Think of the dangerous criminals she might be sharing a cell with."

Jane walked in, and Elsie moved over, making room for her on the couch while they filled Jane in on what they knew.

And the more they talked, the more Elsie dreaded what she knew would have to be done. Someone would have to go to L.A. and fetch Lydia. And someone needed to apologize to Will and try to repay him. The thought made her want to vomit because she knew it would have to be her.

Jane squeezed her hand. "I know what you're thinking, Elsie Bennet. We'll take care of this together."

"Okay."

***

Gianna stared and stared at the video surveillance they were about to hand over to the police. An officer was supposed to stop by for it soon, now that they had suspects they'd arrested and could compare to the video. He wasn't surprised to hear they'd found Jeff. But Lydia Bennet? It hadn't taken long for him to drag her down.

"I'm sorry, Will. This is my fault."

Will's head whipped around. "Gianna, how is it your fault?"

"This is Jeff getting back at us for putting him in jail. And it could have easily been me driving that night. I could be the one with my license revoked."

"Gianna." Will bent down to look her in the eyes. "Jeff is an idiot. A dangerous idiot. He may very well go back to jail because of this and I wouldn't sleep any less over it. But, I actually don't think this prank is about the car accident. Lydia Bennet is Jane and Elsie's little sister, and he put her up to this to hurt me."

"How does Jeff know the Bennets?" Gianna's head tilted, her face showing a disappointed frown. "You've been keeping things from me."

Will sighed. "Jeff showed up in Meryton and latched himself onto the Bennets. He's like a bad rash I can't get rid of."

"I'm so glad he got caught for this. Can you imagine what else he might try if he'd gotten away with it?"

"You have more faith in the judicial system than I do. We'll be lucky if he gets more than a small fine. But I'll start parking in the garage again. I called an auction house. They'll store Dad's Bentley for us until it goes to the highest bidder."

Gianna patted his shoulder. "It's long overdue. But that's not our only problem here. What are you going to do for poor Lydia Bennet? I keep picturing myself in her situation."

Will stiffened. He kept hearing that muffled giggle in his head. One he now realized was Lydia, gleefully helping Jeff slash his tires. He wasn't feeling much sympathy, only disgust. But by the time the cop showed up for the surveillance video, he knew the anger he felt inside wouldn't fix this.

Lydia was convinced he was the bad guy, that Jeff was merely a victim. Changing that perspective was the only way to make this right. He called up a lawyer friend and convinced him to take her case and help her make a good plea deal. Then he posted her bail. He couldn't bring himself to meet with her though. He didn't want to know if she was grateful for his help or resentful. Honestly, it didn't matter.

CHAPTER 21 ♥ ANONYMOUS BENEFACTOR

Lydia's incessant humming while she straightened her hair in the hotel bathroom was about to drive Elsie insane. They'd driven all the way here to rescue her, only to find out she was fine.

Her bail had been posted, she'd gotten her phone and car back, and she was sooo glad she wouldn't miss her audition after all. She just needed to get that annoying meeting with her lawyer out of the way first.

"Is this a public defender we're meeting?" Elsie asked, trying another tack to get the information Lydia insisted on not sharing.

"I don't think so. Richer than that. I hope it means he's good."

"Who is paying him?" Jane asked. She exchanged glances with Elsie. None of this made any sense.

"Not me. But I can't tell you more than that. I'm just mad he won't help Jeff. His bail hasn't even been posted. I've texted Denny, like, a million times, but he's not answering me."

Elsie rubbed the aching spot in the middle of her forehead. "Jeff doesn't need help. This is a mess of his own making. And you! How could you do this, Lydia?"

Lydia turned to them, her face turning into a rehearsed mask. "I admit to nothing. They totally searched my car illegally."

Elsie jumped up from the bed, but Jane gripped her arm. "Don't kill her yet. We have to return her to Mom and Dad first."

"They searched your car?" Elsie asked with sarcastic pity. "How terrible for you. What about the car with the spray paint all over it?"

Lydia went back into the bathroom, her calm making Elsie more enraged. "You can't come along if you're going to freak out like that, Elsie. I thought you wanted to meet my lawyer with me."

She did want to meet Lydia's lawyer, though a part of her wished he'd turn out to be terrible and Lydia would get what she deserved.

"Aren't you the least bit sorry?" Elsie couldn't help adding as they left together to go to the hotel elevator.

Lydia turned. "Saying sorry would be admitting guilt. But hypothetically, if I'd done what they say I did, I would probably wish I hadn't done it."

"That's not an apology," Elsie glared at her sister as she stepped into the elevator and stabbed the lobby button with her finger. "Wishing you hadn't gotten caught is not the same as being sorry. You're wrong about Will. He didn't deserve this. Not that anyone deserves this."

Lydia didn't respond, though she squirmed a little.

They parted ways in the parking lot, and Elsie let Jane drive while she pondered the situation. Most likely, Lydia would get a huge fine and avoid jail time … if she pleaded guilty. But the stubborn girl would never turn on Jeff.

Jane followed Lydia's car to a very nice law firm called Taylor, White, and Associates. Definitely too nice to handle petty crime. Who was paying for this? And why?

The professionally dressed girl at the front desk offered them complimentary waters and directed them to sit and wait. Within a few minutes, a guy with salt-and-pepper hair introduced himself as Andy White and led them into his office.

"Lydia, let's get right to this. The D.A.'s office has no interest in taking this to court, though they certainly have enough evidence that they could. My job is to help you make a good plea deal so you can put this behind you. I'm going to show you the evidence against you and then tell you what they've offered. Okay?"

They all leaned forward as he laid out several black and white pictures of two people in hoodies in front of what Elsie assumed was Will's house. It was definitely his car. She winced at the close up of what they'd done to it.

"Lydia, you and Jeffrey Wickham were wearing hoodies like this the night you were arrested. The spray paint in your car is a color match to the spray paint on Fitzwilliam Darcy's car."

Lydia snorted, interrupting him. "Sorry, I didn't know Will's name was Fitzwilliam. It's so … him."

Andy stared Lydia down while Elsie wished she could crawl under the desk and die.

"Continuing on. The pocket knife found on Jeffrey Wickham is the right type for the slashes on Darcy's tires. And Jeff had a little bit of dog poop on the bottom of his shoe, and while they didn't test it against the pile left on the Darcy's doorstep, they likely could get a match."

"Dog poop?" Jane gasped. "And you slashed his tires?"

Lydia stared at the floor. Like a good criminal, she'd said as little as possible.

"They're throwing out DUI of marijuana thing. That was just a reason to bring you in until they'd figured out what you'd done. But if you agree to plead guilty to the rest, I can get this reduced to an infraction. No jail time. Your benefactor has agreed to pay the five-hundred-dollar fine and you'd be free to go."

"And what about Jeff?" Lydia asked.

"We discussed this on the phone, Lydia. He's on his own. Refusing this to try to help him is foolish."

"Jeff and I agreed we're not saying anything. We're innocent." Lydia crossed her arms, sitting stiffly in her chair.

Andy leaned forward, looking disappointed in her. "Then I need to show you this."

He slid a sheet of paper across the desk. It was a facsimile of a handwritten letter, with Jeff's signature at the bottom. Lydia picked it up and studied it, her face turning from stubborn to beet red and then to a blotchy white. "Someone else wrote this," she said, flinging it back on the table. "He wouldn't say that."

Jane picked it up next, and while Elsie couldn't wait to see what the weasel had done, she was dying to know something else first. "What benefactor?" she asked. "Why is someone helping her?"

Andy shook his head. "That's not something I can discuss."

Elsie sighed and leaned over to read along with Jane. In true Jeff Wickham form, his confession was a detailed explanation of how it was all Lydia's idea along with a heartfelt apology for taking part in it.

"This letter is part of his plea deal. Lydia, if you refuse yours, and this is the only story the judge sees … there won't be much I can do to help you."

Elsie held her breath, but finally, Lydia nodded. "Okay. I'll take it." She sniffed. "Jeff said we wouldn't get caught. And then when we got pulled over, he told me everything would be fine. We just needed to both keep our mouths shut. He said the cops were too busy to care about little stuff like this."

Elsie was about to say something, but a look from Jane silenced her. And she was right. Anything Elsie said at this point would sound like an I-Told-You-So.

The Lydia who left the law office was a much-subdued version of the girl Elsie had always known. But she was still determined to go to her audition. They wished her luck and watched her drive off.

***

"It's done."

"Thank you, Andy." Will gripped his phone, so relieved to put the whole thing behind him. With his car repainted and his porch cleaned off, he could hopefully forget about it.

"I checked on Jeff Wickham's case. He also got a plea deal. Who has time for anything else? But his fine is higher and he'll be on probation for a year."

"Not much of a plea deal, if you ask me."

Andy laughed. "Well, he didn't have me as his lawyer."

"Send me your bill and don't hold back." Will leaned back in his chair and put his feet up on the desk. If Gianna saw him she'd tsk and make him put his feet down, but she'd gone to lunch with friends.

"I'll bill you for every second."

Will laughed and was about to hang up when Andy said, "I do have a question if you don't mind me asking."

Dang, he'd been hoping to avoid this. "I may plead the fifth."

"Understandably. So, Lydia has no criminal record, but she didn't seem particularly sorry or fond of you. Why are you helping her? Is it one of the sisters?"

Will's feet dropped to the floor. "How do you know she has sisters?"

"They were with her today. I liked them much better than my client, I'll tell you that. I think they used up all the sense in the family before Lydia came along."

"Which sisters?" He couldn't just assume it was Elsie and Jane, though they seemed the most likely.

"Uh, Jane and Alice, I think."

"Do you mean Elsie?"

"Yes, that was it." There was a pause, while Andy chuckled. "Interested in Elsie?"

"I didn't say that."

"She was very curious about Lydia's benefactor."

"But you didn't tell her."

"I promised I wouldn't. As far as I know, Lydia's kept her promise not to say anything either."

Will relaxed. "Thank you, Andy."

He hung up and mulled the situation over. Will had told himself this was about convincing Lydia he wasn't a bad guy, but just the mention of Elsie had him unnerved. He still cared about her. He still wished things had been different. And if he was being honest, the real reason he'd bailed out Lydia was because if he didn't, it would have likely fallen to Elsie's shoulders. He was happy he'd spared her that, even if she'd never know it was him.

***

"I can do this." Elsie rolled her shoulders back and stared at her phone. She'd decided showing up on Will's doorstep would be a bit much, even if she knew where he lived. She could call that lawyer and ask him nicely for the address, but considering her sister had vandalized the place, she doubted he'd want to give her information on Will.

But she couldn't let the whole thing go without doing something. She'd falsely accused him of wronging Jeff, and then her own sister had taken it about five hundred steps further. Even if he abruptly hung up on her, she needed him to know how sorry she was. He deserved that much.

She scrolled down to Will's number, which she only had from a group text with Charlie and Jane, and pressed it, closing her eyes tightly shut while it rang. Leaving a message would be nice. In fact, after three rings she started preparing one in her mind.

"Hello?"

The sound of his voice sent her heartbeat into overdrive. Her throat dried up and she swallowed hard.

"Will, this is Elsie. I wanted to say how sorry I am for what

Lydia's done, and I want to pay you for the damage. I know insurance covers things like that but I'm sure it affected the value of your car, you know, not having its original paint anymore. Anyway, I just wanted to say I'm sorry, and I take responsibility for what happened." She rubbed her forehead with her palm and waited for him to say something.

The three seconds before he answered seemed like an eternity.

"Elsie, you don't owe me anything. I know it was Lydia and not you. At least, I hope not." There was a hint of humor in his voice that made her feel slightly better.

"I'm sorry I ever believed a word of what Jeff said." Just the mention of his name turned the whole thing more awkward than it already was. "Okay, well—"

"Wait. Would you like to come over for dinner? I could introduce you to my sister Gianna."

"That's so nice. Um, how did you know I'm in L.A.?" She glanced around, wondering if he had some kind of GPS on his phone that told him she was calling from close by.

"Oh, I ... uh ... I figured you came to help Lydia and that's why you were calling. Are you in Meryton?"

"No, you're right. I'm in L.A. Jane's with me."

"You should both come."

Elsie's stomach began to flutter with the possibility, but Jane was coming out of the bathroom right then and Elsie lost courage. "We're actually meeting Mary at some vegan restaurant tonight. But, thank you." She quickly ended the call and slipped the phone behind her, awash with conflicting emotions. Relief, disappointment, regret. There was no way she could just go over to Will's for dinner like everything was not weird, but oh, how she wished she could.

"Who was that?" Jane came over, rubbing her wet hair with a hand towel.

"Um, Lydia."

"Then why is your face all ... I don't know ... glowy?"

"Because Lydia got the main role?"

"Now I know you're lying." Jane sat down next to her and struck out for the phone, grabbing it before Elsie could stop her.

"No!" Elsie tried to take it back, but Jane ran to the bathroom and shut the door on her.

Darn Jane and her lightning-fast reflexes. Why couldn't she take

136

a long shower like a normal person? Maybe she wouldn't be able to figure out who the number belonged to. Elsie checked the doorknob, but of course, Jane had locked it.

"Ah, ha!" Jane declared after a minute, her voice muffled through the door. "I had a wild hunch and I was right."

She came out with the phone behind her back. "What did you mean by, 'but thank you'? Did Will invite you to something and you turned him down?"

"We're meeting Mary for dinner."

Jane grinned. "No, Lydia and I are meeting Mary for dinner. You can stop complaining about chickpeas and tofu and call him back right now. Whatever it is, don't you dare turn him down."

Elsie shook her head. "I can't do that. I already told him—" Jane tapped on the screen and put the phone to her ear. "What are you doing? Stop that right now!"

Jane retreated back into the bathroom, though this time with the door open. "Hi, Will. This is Jane."

Elsie paced in front of her, fighting the urge to grab the phone and end the call. But that would only make this look worse. Instead, she sent non-verbal threats Jane's way while Jane smiled and ignored her, as if Elsie were throwing out jazz hands instead of shaking fists.

"It's good to hear from you, too. Mmhmm." Jane turned away, so as not to be distracted. "Well, I really need to go see my sister, Mary, but we're happy to spare Elsie for the evening. She's all yours."

When had Jane become so sneaky? So meddling? It was like she'd stolen a page out of Elsie's playbook. If this was what it felt like, Elsie vowed to never meddle again. She frantically began ripping apart her suitcase, looking for her most flattering pair of jeans. All she had were comfortable, clean-up-after-your-sister type outfits. She hoped he wasn't expecting her to dress formally.

Jane scribbled down something on the hotel notepad and hung up. "Let me help you." She went to her own suitcase and pulled out a navy blouse with little white polka-dots. The keyhole neckline tied at the top in a cute little bow. It was very much a Jane shirt and not an Elsie one.

"No, I'm just going in my T-shirt and jeans." Elsie pulled out one of their new T-shirts and studied it. The soft gray material looked great against the gold foil arrows running diagonally across the front. "This is me being me." Elsie looked down at Jane's beaded gold sandals. "But I'm stealing those. Please?"

Jane took them off and handed them over. "I take it I also owe you my first-born child and I'll be doing your laundry for the next three years?"

"Four years."

Jane put her hands on Elsie's shoulders. "He wouldn't have asked if he didn't want to see you. Will doesn't do anything as an empty gesture. Tell me I'm not right."

Elsie's heart fluttered. Jane was right. He did want to see her. He could have easily thanked her and hung up. Or told Jane they should both go meet with Mary. But he didn't.

CHAPTER 22 ♥ DINNER DATE

Will tried to keep a poker face as he explained the situation to Gianna, but all she heard was the name Elsie, and she grinned, clapping in excitement.

"She's really coming here? Tonight?"

"Well, if she doesn't talk herself out of it. I have a feeling Jane is trying to play matchmaker against her will. But then, every date I've had with Elsie has been against her will, so what's one more?"

"You have a very morbid sense of humor. Now follow me to the kitchen, and let's get this dinner started." Gianna wheeled out of the den and over to the kitchen. Within seconds she had a counter full of ingredients and a heated wok on the stove.

"Start the rice cooker and then cut up this chicken. I'm getting the marinade ready."

They worked together, prepping for something he was trying very hard not to think too much about. What did Elsie think of him now? Maybe he was being cruel to himself, letting his hopes raise again, only to be disappointed. It was vanity to think Elsie would ever like him as more than an unfortunate acquaintance.

The doorbell rang just as Gianna dropped the meat in the pan, the loud sizzle almost making him think he'd imagined the ringing sound. But then he heard it again. He and Jane had decided on six. It was only five-forty. Maybe they only had the one vehicle and had to drop Elsie early. Regardless, he dashed to the door, not wanting to keep her waiting.

But Caroline stood on the front step. She smiled and came up to kiss his cheek. "I hope you don't mind me stopping in. There's nothing to eat at my house and my favorite show has been canceled because of the President's stupid press conference. Like anyone cares about a little tornado in Oklahoma."

She breezed past him, her heavy purse whacking him in the arm on the way in. Will snapped out of his shock and followed her into the kitchen, thinking up possible solutions. He peered around Caroline, to meet Gianna's eyes. "Do something!" he mouthed.

Gianna wiped her hands on a towel and smiled at whatever Caroline was yammering on about. He could almost see the wheels turning in Gianna's head before she spoke.

"So, Caroline. Would you be a dear, and help me package up two servings of this? I was just talking to Mrs. Long, our neighbor, and her husband broke his foot last week. He usually does the cooking at their house. I bet they would love some of this."

"Yes, but…" Caroline looked at the stir-fry hungrily, and Gianna slid a plate towards her. "By all means, have a quick bite first. I just don't want to wait too long or they'll resort to eating something disgusting, like ravioli out of a can."

Caroline shuddered. "Yes, that would be horrible." She filled her plate with rice and veggies and ate quickly while Gianna got out plastic tubs and portioned out the food.

Gianna took the opportunity to glare at Will. A look that meant he was about to owe her big time.

"Caroline, I'm so glad you're here. I was thinking after we drop off the food… I need a new dress for this charity thing I'll be attending, and you know how salespeople can be when I wheel through the door."

"Say no more." Caroline took a last bite and chewed quickly. "I'll take care of everything. And if they are even the least bit snooty, you just watch me make a scene. I'm kind of hoping for it. I haven't chewed out a store manager in a while."

Will bit his lip to keep the laughter in. He carried out the bag of food Gianna had prepared and handed it to Gianna after placing her wheelchair in the backseat of Caroline's car. Gianna grabbed his collar and pulled him down to her level. "Make this time count, Will."

He kissed her cheek, ignoring the pressure her words added. "Have fun."

"Sure you don't want to come with?" Caroline asked.

"I'll be fine. Thank you, though."

He released the breath he'd been holding as they drove around the corner. The Long's shared a backyard fence with them. Kind and smart Gianna had picked excuses that both helped someone and got her and Gianna out of sight quick. She was a better sister than he deserved. He hoped Gianna really did need a dress, but he also hoped she hadn't really encountered rude sales people in the past. That was awful. As annoying as Caroline could be, she was fiercely loyal to Gianna. Some poor salesperson, whether they deserved it or not, was about to wish they didn't work in sales.

***

The front door was massive. Elsie stared up at the polished wood and then down at the curved, wrought iron handles. Will Darcy was behind this door, waiting for her. It took another minute for her to work up the courage to knock. When she did, he answered almost immediately, catching her off guard.

"Hi." She stood there stupidly, just staring at his handsome face. He looked nervous.

"Come in."

She stepped into the foyer, immediately smelling something delicious.

"I hope you're hungry. Gianna made a ton of food." He led the way into the kitchen, but it was still just the two of them. He got out two plates and put them on the table, before moving back to get glasses and forks.

Only two plates. She looked from the plates to him and he rubbed the back of his neck, looking away. "Sorry, Gianna ran off to go shopping with Caroline." His mouth closed abruptly, as if there was more to that story.

Or maybe he realized how it sounded. Obviously, Gianna wasn't that interested in meeting her. Elsie would not allow herself to be offended by that. Who knew how little Gianna even knew of her. Maybe she wanted to give them some alone time. No, that possibility was too awesomely terrifying to consider. She couldn't let her mind go there either.

"Can I help with anything?" She put her purse on the back of a stool and clasped her hands together.

"Oh, yes. There's lemonade in the fridge. Would you bring it over?"

She got out an elegant glass pitcher filled with what looked like fresh-squeezed lemonade. Lemon slices were floating on top. She wondered if Gianna had prepared this too.

"We have two lemon trees outside that overproduce this time of year. You should take some home with you."

"Thank you." She bit her lip. He was being so polite. She kind of missed the Will with the flashing eyes, the one who told her she had soda all down her shirt. Or the one who had grabbed her up and kissed her in the library. Now that image was tap dancing across her consciousness while Will served her rice and stir-fry. She met his eyes and prayed he had no mind-reading powers.

"Is that enough?"

She stared down at her plate. "Yes. It's perfect." She picked up her fork and took a bite. Wonderful, though she barely registered it. Her mind couldn't be bothered with trivial things like swallowing or breathing normally.

She reached for the pitcher and carefully poured herself a glass. "Would you like some?"

He nodded.

The pitcher was heavy, and to be honest, clunky. She regretted her offer as soon as she had the thing hovering over his glass. She poured slowly and the first ounce or two went in fine, but then a lemon slice blocked up the spout for a second, and when it moved, lemonade gushed out, missing the glass and spilling across the table and straight onto his lap.

He yelped in surprise and jumped out of his chair.

Elsie put down the pitcher and scooted out, running for a kitchen towel that was sitting on the counter. "Oh, Will. I'm so sorry." Her stomach clenched, and she held out the towel to him, afraid to meet his eyes. It looked like he'd wet his pants.

He took the towel and brushed off his slacks, while she went back, searching the drawers until she found the washcloths. She wet one in the sink and began cleaning off the table. Almost all the lemonade had made it onto his pants. There wasn't even much on the floor. She so needed to go home and pretend she'd never met him.

"Elsie, it's okay." Will put the towel down next to her and touched her arm. She turned to look at him, expecting to see annoyance, but he only looked amused.

"Sit and eat. I'm going to change. I'm overdressed anyway."

It was true. With his slacks and button-down crisp shirt, he made her jeans and T-shirt seem grungy.

His hand didn't move from her arm. "That came out wrong. You look nice. You always do. I just feel like I'm ready for a computer programming convention. All I need is my pocket protector."

She stared at him in shock.

"That was a joke, Elsie."

"I know."

"Next time, I'll think up a better one."

Before she could think of a rebuttal, he walked out, only slightly waddling on his way. Great, now he thought she didn't find him funny, and she'd probably ruined five-hundred-dollar pants. She grabbed up the washrag and rinsed it out, adding dish soap while waiting for the water to warm. That lemonade would turn everything into a sticky mess. There was no way she'd sit back down until every drip was accounted for.

***

So, this was going well. Will laughed to himself as he peeled off his slacks. He should have taken the pitcher out of her hands. He knew she was struggling with it. But he didn't want to come off as a control freak so he'd let her continue… to pour lemonade all over the place.

Would they ever find a way to just be themselves? He unbuttoned his shirt and placed it back on a hanger. He'd only worn it for thirty minutes and the lemonade miraculously hadn't touched it. After changing, he jogged downstairs. Elsie was on her hands and knees scrubbing the floor. He didn't want to embarrass her further, so he waited until she got up to rinse the rag again. He should have cleaned up with her before going to change. He should have told her how much Gianna wanted to meet her. He should have complimented her on how she looked when she first walked in.

Regrets would not help this situation though, so he came in and they ate their now cold food.

"You want a tour of the house?" he asked when she was done eating. He took their plates to the sink and led the way. There were a lot of rooms they rarely used anymore. Mostly extra bedrooms and bathrooms. A maid came once a week to clean and dust. It was way more than Gianna could maintain on her own, no matter how much she wanted to.

After taking her through most of the house, they picked lemons in the backyard, and she put a bag of them by her purse in the kitchen.

He saved the basketball court for last and watched Elsie's face as she walked in.

"This is awesome."

"Do you play?"

She scuffed her gold sandal across the floor. "I'm not exactly dressed for it."

"That wasn't my question."

She gave him the challenging look he'd grown quite fond of. "I played in high school, although that's not saying much. They took anyone who had the grades for it."

"We could play barefoot."

He could tell she didn't believe him, so he took off his shoes and socks and walked over to get a ball off the rack.

A glance back told him she'd slipped off her sandals and moved to follow him. He dribbled a few times, getting close enough for her to reach out and try to steal the ball, but he moved out of range each time.

She rolled her eyes and jogged away, placing herself under the basket. When he made his shot, she grabbed the rebound and dribbled off to the side, preparing to make a shot.

It really wasn't fair. He could block her just by standing in front of her. Putting his hands up only added to the impossibility of getting the ball over him.

She dribbled left and faked right, but he anticipated it and moved with her. She didn't give up. She put her left hand to his stomach and gave him a saucy little grin, continuing to dribble with her right hand while nudging him away. The contact was just enough to throw him off his game, and the next time she faked, she got around him and made a shot.

He'd never played with someone he was attracted to. It added a whole different dimension to the game. He grabbed the rebound and welcomed a close defense. He dribbled for longer than was necessary, letting her come in close and try to reach around him while he dribbled the ball behind his back. She pushed against his ribs with her shoulder, and he laughed.

"Um, you're totally fouling me."

"Whatever, don't be a baby." She hugged him around the middle, finally reaching the ball and knocking it away. It was all he could do not to grab her up and continue where they'd left off in the library a few weeks ago. But he wasn't sure where competition ended and flirting began. The two were so intertwined.

They played to ten points, enough that they could stop before getting too sweaty. He won by four points, something she pretended to be miffed about.

They headed over to the mini fridge in the corner where he kept water bottles.

He handed her one and drank half of his in one guzzle.

"I'm dying for a hair tie right now." She lifted her hair with one hand, shaking it up off her neck while she drank from her water bottle.

"Can't you put it in a knot?" He demonstrated with some swirling motion that had her giving him an amused glare.

"With some bobby pins or a pencil, yeah. But I can't just twirl my hair and make it stay in place."

She put her water bottle down and lifted her hair up again, twisting it around her finger. Having never had long hair, he could only imagine how bothersome it would feel against a hot neck.

When she turned away from him, he couldn't resist pouring a little water down the back of her shirt.

She shrieked and turned to face him, her face full of shock. "I can't believe you." Her eyes went to her water bottle, and he took a step back.

"I was helping you cool off."

She picked up her water bottle and took a step toward him. "It's always nice to help someone in need."

He sprinted out of her reach, and she followed, sloshing water as she ran. He looked back just as she slipped on the slick wood floor and went down on her bum.

She rubbed her backside. "Oh, that's karma, right there."

He came over and sat down next to her. "Are you okay?"

She winced. "Nothing's broken. But yeah, that hurts. I slipped on the water intended for you." She picked up her water bottle and sloshed the last little bit across his chest, laughing through her pain.

"Feel better now?"

"Slightly."

He couldn't help it. He leaned in, his lips getting just a taste of hers before— "Ahem."

They pulled away from each other and looked over to the door. Caroline was leaning against the door jam, her arms crossed. "Sorry to interrupt."

CHAPTER 23 ♥ "GO HOME, CAROLINE."

Will jumped to his feet and held out a hand for Elsie to do the same. He was painfully aware that they were both barefoot, and he had a water stain down his front, while Elsie had one down her back. He didn't give two hoots what Caroline thought of it, of him acting this way, but this had been his and Elsie's moment, and now it was over.

Caroline eyed Elsie warily. "Gianna and I will be in the kitchen. We found her the perfect dress."

Elsie stepped away from him and walked toward her sandals against the wall. If she'd just look at him, maybe he could convey how sorry he was for the interruption.

He wracked his brain for the right thing to say. Anything would be better than nothing, but she left the room before he could figure out what that anything was. He gathered up the now empty water bottles and followed her to the kitchen.

Gianna tugged on his sleeve. "Hey, genius. Check your phone occasionally." He wasn't even sure where his phone was.

Gianna put on a warm smile for Elsie. "I'm so glad to finally meet you."

Elsie came over and bent down to give Gianna a hug. "And I'm excited to meet you."

"Gianna, where should I hang this up?" Caroline lifted up the garment bag, showing off the glittering ivory dress inside.

"Thank you, Caroline. If you'd put it in my closet, that would be so helpful." Gianna turned back to Elsie. "So, how did dinner go?"

Elsie blushed. "It was delicious, thank you."

"She especially enjoyed the lemonade," Will added. For the first time since they'd hopped off the gym floor, Elsie looked at him and smiled.

"Do you have room for dessert?" Gianna asked. "We have lots of ice cream in the freezer." She glanced up at Will. "We could eat while we watch a movie."

Caroline breezed back in. "Oh, I know the perfect one. These two angels fall in love while on assignment."

Normally, Will hated sappy romantic movies, but he saw the way Elsie's eyes lit up at the mention of it.

"Great, I'll rent it." He went into the media room and found the movie on one of the apps. He had it all primed when the three girls came in with their bowls of ice cream.

"Here's yours." Caroline handed him a bowl and plopped down on the leather couch next to him before Elsie could. Elsie raised an eyebrow, but she went to the other end to sit next to Gianna, who had parked her wheelchair next to it.

On nights when it was only the two of them, Will usually helped Gianna out of her wheelchair and onto the couch, but she'd given a slight shake of her head when they'd first come in, letting him know she was fine in her chair.

He was not starting this movie with Caroline usurping his date. "Swap me seats, Caroline. I like to be in the middle."

"In the middle of what?" she asked coyly.

"The middle of the screen," he snapped back.

She gave a little pout and moved over as he stood up and took her spot.

Caroline snuggled back into him. "I'm having ice cream envy. That chocolate chip looks so good." She swiped a little out of his bowl and gave a satisfied sigh. He turned to Elsie, determined to get the night back on track, but she was chatting with Gianna. He pointed the remote at the screen. Time to start this stupid movie.

***

Elsie tried to enjoy the movie, but she felt stupid for being there. The look Caroline had given her when she walked in had one clear message. BACK OFF. Elsie never walked away from a challenge, but she was also highly practical. And it was obvious that while annoying, Caroline was a permanent fixture in their household, with power to wield. Just look at what she'd done to Charlie and Jane. The blame percentages kept changing in her head. How much was Charlie's decision? How much Will's? How much Caroline's?

She'd read the letter from Will so many times she had most of it memorized. *I had high hopes for Jane and Charlie. He was afraid a long distance relationship wouldn't work, as it's been a disaster for him in the past. The only thing I urged him to do was let Jane know.*

One thing she'd come to understand about Will was that he never lied, though that didn't always mean he saw things the same way she did. If what he said was true, why had Charlie strung Jane along if he had no interest in long-distance relationships?

Will's arm was warm against hers, his hand resting between their seats, an invitation to hold hands if she so wished. But she couldn't do it with Caroline's constant surveillance. This night had been a roller coaster of ups and downs. And tomorrow she'd return to Meryton, while he stayed here. She would not be Jane. She would not blindly trust that everything would work out, only to be disappointed.

As the credits rolled, she stood up. "I should get going. It was so nice to meet you, Gianna." She gave her a goodbye hug before turning to Caroline. "Always nice to see you, Caroline." Under the circumstances, there was no choice but to hug it out with her too. Caroline pulled back from the hug, her smile so wooden it could pass as a grimace.

Will stood waiting. "I'll walk you out."

Butterflies gathered in her stomach as his hand moved to her lower back, searing her with his touch.. They left the movie room, and she gathered up her purse and the bag of lemons, hugging them to her.

Her body was so in tune to his every move next to her. She couldn't forget that small kiss, enough of one for her to crave the real thing. She needed to get out of here. She couldn't be falling for Will Darcy. Not when she still felt like an interloper in his fancy house.

She unlocked her car door and reached across to place her things in the passenger seat. Straightening, Will was right there, standing just a foot away, looking concerned.

"I'm sorry our water fight was cut short."

She bit back a grin. "I'm sorry I doused you in lemonade."

"Are you leaving tomorrow?" He rested his arm across the top of her open car door, his fingers reaching out to brush against her shoulder. He wanted to kiss her. She knew it as clearly as she knew she wanted him to. But why did he want this? They were so different, weren't they?

"Yes, we're driving back in the morning."

"Can I call you?" He was moving in for the kill. Leaning in. He was a lion, and she was a terrified gazelle, caught in his gaze.

"Sure." She sank into the driver's seat before he reached her and put her keys in the ignition with a shaking hand. She glanced up at him once more. If he was disappointed in her sudden retreat, he hid it well.

"Bye, Will. I had a great time. Thanks so much."

"Goodnight, Elsie."

He shut her door and she backed out of his driveway, her nerves feeling like the frayed ends of a rope.

***

Caroline and Gianna were laughing in the kitchen when he walked back in and it only rankled him more. "Go home, Caroline." Why hadn't he said it when Elsie was here?

"Well, someone's in a grumpy mood." Caroline rolled her eyes and went to get her shopping bags off the far counter. "I take it Elsie Bennet didn't give you the sendoff you were hoping for. Why are you playing around with her anyway? You said you hated her. That she was judgmental and rude. Oh, and fairly ordinary. That part I can agree on. She's like a before picture in a makeover spread."

Gianna started to defend Elsie, but Will stopped her with a shake of his head before turning to Caroline. "You don't feel the least bit hypocritical calling her judgmental and rude right now?"

Caroline smirked. "You said it first."

"Yes, I did. You have this tendency to hyper-focus on any girl I've ever been interested in, so I downplayed Elsie's good qualities and mentioned the bad ones. That was a mistake. But I've never 'played around' with anyone. Everything I do is with intention, and I plan to pursue Elsie Bennet whether you like her or not."

Caroline's chin raised a fraction and she stalked over to the entryway with her bags. "I see I've touched a nerve. We've always been good friends, and I'm sorry if my teasing was too much. Good night, all."

Will took a deep breath, letting go of some of his anger and went to give Caroline a hug, though she couldn't hug him back with her arms full of shopping bags.

"You're always welcome here, Caroline."

"Sure I am," she murmured. "You just told me to leave."

"Well, you tried to upstage my date."

Gianna came up behind them. "Be nice, you two."

Caroline leaned over and kissed Gianna on the cheek. "Bye, gorgeous. Try to keep this brother of yours in line."

"I always try."

They gave twin sighs of relief when the door closed and it was the two of them once more.

"Do I get to hear about your date?" Gianna asked.

"Someday."

She laughed. "Yeah, that's what I figured."

***

Thankfully, Jane and Lydia were still at dinner when Elsie got back to the hotel. Jane texted to say they were on their way to a poetry slam with Mary. Elsie sent her condolences and used the time to shower and try to relax, alone with her thoughts.

She already missed Will. She felt like she'd only scratched the surface of who he was, and the deeper she saw, the more she realized how much she was still missing. Sadly, she'd probably never get to see it all. How could a long distance relationship work if Jane and Charlie couldn't figure it out? Will would never be happy in Meryton, and moving to L.A.? That wasn't about to happen. She had to think about something else. Work would do.

She wrapped a towel around her wet hair and sat on one of the beds in her pajamas, checking to see how far behind they were getting on T-shirt orders. December was usually their biggest month and things would only get crazier the closer they got to Christmas.

Her phone rang, and she was surprised to see Charlotte's name pop up. Elsie felt a twinge of guilt. Here she was in L.A. and she hadn't even thought of stopping in to see Charlotte.

"Hi, Char. How are you?"

"I'm great. Sorry it's been so long since we talked. How is Lydia? I heard about the … um … incident."

"You did? How?"

"Your mom called Collin, hysterical. She said she was worried about all of you. She wanted him to check on things and help. He promised he'd look into it, but he was worried about his reputation. He's always worried about his reputation. So, he delegated it to me, which I'm pretty sure you would prefer. Do you need money?"

His reputation. Jerk. If Elsie was in a dark pit and Collin was holding a flashlight at the top, she'd still tell him to go away.

"We're fine. It's all settled, and we're leaving in the morning."

"Would you have time to come over for breakfast? I'd love the company."

"Oh, I don't know. Jane and I need to get back and catch up on T-shirt orders."

"Please, Elsie." For the first time in the conversation, Charlotte didn't sound self-assured and business-like. "I won't keep you long. I just need to talk to someone who's not sending me off on errands."

"So, you're working for Collin? I thought he got you a job at a salon?"

"I do both. The salon is very competitive. The more experienced stylists get to choose their clients and hours. I work around them."

"Ah, that makes sense. Dare I ask how things are going with you and Collin?"

Charlotte gave a sad little laugh. "Eh, I'm more of a personal assistant now. Girlfriend is more of an honorary title to keep the gold diggers away. I'm not sure Collin is capable of loving anyone as much as he loves himself. But he treats me well and Catherine De Bourgh is very pleased with me. I've freed up a lot of her time. It's a lot cheaper for her to pay me to do what she charges Collin to think she's doing."

"Is he getting ripped off?"

"Oh, no. Catherine still gives him financial guidance. She just doesn't micromanage him the way she did in the beginning. Now she micromanages me. Don't be surprised if she barges in on our breakfast tomorrow. Please come. I'll text you the address."

152

CHAPTER 24 ♥ PERSONAL SPACE

Charlotte's apartment building was in Beverly Hills, with a gorgeous trio of water fountains flowing in front and a kind doorman in uniform waiting to assist Elsie inside.

They'd agreed on six-thirty, and Charlotte had everything set out and ready when Elsie came inside. Two glasses of orange juice, a stack of pancakes in the middle of the table, and fluffy scrambled eggs already on each plate. Charlotte had always been a good cook. Even when she was younger, Charlotte was the one who did most of the cooking for her family.

Charlotte grabbed Elsie's hands. "I'm so happy you're here. You have to catch me up on all the Meryton gossip."

Meryton gossip? That had always been Charlotte's forte. Elsie didn't pay attention to much outside her own family, and Charlotte already knew about Lydia. Will's face popped into her consciousness, and she pushed him aside. She didn't need an I-told-you-so from Charlotte about him.

Charlotte sat down and served herself a pancake. "Come on, Elsie. Dig deep. Have you seen my mother at the library?"

"Of course. She misses you. Oh, and she said your little sister got a job at Dairy Queen."

"Yeah, Mariah texted me about that yesterday. She has a crush on one of her co-workers. He has a locker next to her at school, but she says he doesn't know she exists."

"Yay, high school. Don't miss that." Elsie put a swirl of syrup on her pancake and took a bite. So good. "Char, you should've been a chef."

"No way. I'd have to work nights and weekends for the rest of my life. Plus, there's no money in it."

That was Charlotte. Ever practical.

Elsie set down her fork. "I was wondering something. When you asked if we needed money ... Collin didn't hire a lawyer for Lydia, did he?"

Charlotte gave her a puzzled look. "I thought you said everything was resolved."

"It is. Never mind." So Collin was not the mysterious benefactor. Elsie went back to her working theory that it was some eccentric contact Lydia had picked up in pursuit of an acting career. And that made Elsie about ninety percent less curious about it.

Charlotte's phone chirped and she picked it up, her forehead wrinkling. "Catherine's stopping by. She wants to inspect the dress I bought for a charity event we're going to. I talked her into letting me pick it out, but it has to meet with her approval. You should've seen her go bonkers at Collin's tuxedo fitting. She said a first tuxedo is a momentous occasion in a man's life."

"She's inspecting the dress you'll be wearing?"

"Uh-huh. Better scarf down your food and then we'll go try it on. If I wait 'til she gets here, she'll follow me into my bedroom and criticize my underwear choices."

Elsie choked on her bite of egg, trying not to laugh so she could clear her throat. "Can't wait."

They ate as fast as they could. Elsie helped Charlotte clean up, carrying everything to the kitchen where they rushed to wash the dishes and put away leftovers.

"How long do you think we have?" Elsie asked.

"About ten more minutes if traffic is bad. Let's hope a bus breaks down in the middle of the road or something."

Elsie followed her down the hall, and Charlotte pulled a garment bag out of the closet. She set it on the bed and unzipped, revealing a forest green satin ball gown.

Elsie sucked in a breath. "It's gorgeous. I can't believe you get to wear that."

"Me neither. Just one of the perks of the job."

And while being glamorous and hobnobbing with the rich and famous wasn't something Elsie cared about, she could see why it would appeal to Charlotte. This dress was going to make Charlotte's green eyes sparkle like emeralds.

There was an imperious knock at the door.

"Quick. Throw it over my head." Charlotte peeled off her shirt and shimmied out of her expensive new jeans while Elsie picked up the dress and helped Charlotte into it. She zipped up the back as the knocking came again.

"Elsie, will you let her in? I'll be out in a second."

***

After running a few miles on the treadmill, Will took to the basketball court, shooting from the free throw line and running to retrieve his rebounds.

Gianna had been busy doing her physical therapy with Becky, but afterward, she came in and watched.

"Is Elsie returning to Meryton today?"

He turned and dribbled over to her, putting the ball away on the wire shelf against the wall. "Yes."

"Then what's your plan, Romeo?"

Will wiped the sweat from his forehead and threatened to wipe it on her.

She frowned at him, daring him with her eyes to do it. They both knew he wouldn't.

"I'm only trying to help, Will."

She was always trying to help. If he didn't love her so much he'd tell her to stick her pretty little nose in someone else's business. "I don't have a plan, Gianna. Nobody likes me in Meryton. I can't show up there without Charlie, and he's not going back."

"Elsie likes you."

"That's debatable."

Gianna laughed. "She does. However, I don't think she's a fan of Caroline."

"Obviously."

"You should call her."

"I plan to."

"When?"

Will looked over at the clock on the wall. "Not at seven in the morning."

"So send her a text. Start small. Quit worrying about Charlie or planning a trip to Meryton, and woo her properly."

"Did you just say 'woo'?"

155

She turned her wheelchair towards the door, and he followed.

"Woo. As in, woohoo, she'll know you care." She grinned up at him.

Will shook his head, sure Gianna was out of her mind. "What about your love life, Gianna? Dropping off loaves of bread to anyone lately?"

She blushed. "You'll never let me live that one down. But actually, I do have a date for the charity ball coming up."

They entered the kitchen and he sat on a stool. "Who with?"

"Hector Lopez."

Will reached for the fruit bowl in the middle of the island counter and grabbed an apple. "Is this a guy on your basketball team?"

Gianna shook her head. "No, he's actually our UPS guy."

"You asked out the delivery guy? Are you crazy? What do you even know about him?"

She narrowed her eyes. "More than you think. We've been chatting at least once a week at the front door for two years. Two years, Will. I know he loves to go fishing and mountain biking. He sends money to his grandparents in Mexico every month. And he's had a steady girlfriend up until about three months ago. Besides, he asked me out first. I suggested the charity ball because otherwise, I'd have to take you, and you'd complain the whole time."

Will still didn't like her going out with someone he'd never met. But at least it would be a public place. "Is this why you order so much junk online?"

She smiled and turned to look in the fridge. "I never order junk. But yes, I do order things just to see him. I'm pretty sure he knows that."

"Two years, huh. At least we know he has a steady job."

"Text Elsie already."

He walked out with his apple. "I'll think about it." But he pulled out his phone as soon as he was out of sight and sent a quick text, wishing Elsie a safe drive.

***

Catherine's beady eyes missed nothing as she surveyed the dress. She tugged a little on the bodice. "This will need to be taken in or your bosom will get lost in there. Call the seamstress immediately

156

and make sure she can fit you in this week."

"Yes, Catherine." Charlotte's hands fidgeted, but she froze and stood taller when Catherine started messing with the back of the dress.

"You'll need an up-do to show off the detailing back here. Is someone at your salon doing your hair?"

"Yes, Catherine."

Catherine turned to look at Elsie, taking in her T-shirt, jeans, and flip-flops. "I see now why things didn't work between you and Collin."

Elsie wasn't sure how to answer that. Thank you? "I'm not interested in a relationship right now."

"That's right. You have your shirt business with your sister."

Elsie's phone pinged and lit up with a text message. It was sitting on the coffee table between her and Catherine. Elsie reached for it, but not before Catherine leaned over to read the message. The woman's eyes widened in surprise.

"Why is my nephew messaging you?"

Elsie cradled her phone against her chest. She'd finally created a contact for Will last night. Just in time for Catherine to see his name splashed across Elsie's phone.

Charlotte shot her a sympathetic look. "Elsie and I both know Will. He stayed in our hometown with Charlie Bingley for a few weeks."

"And does he send you messages as well, Charlotte? Telling you good morning and hoping you'll have a safe trip?"

"Well, no. I ... I'm not going on any trips." Charlotte glanced at Elsie, an apology in her eyes.

Elsie had been prepared for the unexpected, but this? She couldn't even process her feelings about Will texting so soon. Not with Charlotte's obvious curiosity, and especially not with Catherine's unrepentant snooping. But it was her nephew and it made sense she'd be interested in his love life. Elsie would act like this didn't bother her, for Charlotte's sake.

"Go change, Charlotte. Put it away carefully." Catherine dismissed her with a half a wave. When Charlotte was safely out of the room, she narrowed her eyes at Elsie.

"I thought you weren't interested in a relationship. Maybe you're just not interested in new money. Will is twice the man Collin is without trying. It's in his blood. I admire your taste, but really, you have no business attempting to reel in a Darcy."

"I'm not trying to reel him in—"

"Do you realize the tickets to this event Charlotte's preparing for are ten thousand dollars a person? It's a sold out event. Will and Gianna Darcy will be there. Collin and Charlotte will be there. Anyone who is anyone will be there. But you won't."

"What does that have to do with—?"

"You will return to your one-horse town, taking your delinquent little sister with you, and cease contacting my family. Immediately."

Elsie's mouth dropped open in shock. Okay, never mind. She was not going to let this go. And she was tired of being cut off so Catherine could insult her further. Elsie squared her shoulders and took a step closer, invading Catherine's personal space. "So, when do I get to read your text messages and give you orders, Ms. De Bourgh? I think you're forgetting the fact that I don't work for you, nor do I care what you think of me."

Charlotte walked back in, eyes wide. "Is everything okay?"

"Love you, Char. I gotta go." Elsie went over to give her a hug. "Good luck," she whispered in Charlotte's ear. Then she hightailed it out of there because as much as she'd enjoyed her show of bravado and the woman's shocked reaction, if it came to a hair-pulling fist fight, she wasn't sure she'd win.

When she was safely in the elevator, Elsie pulled out her phone and read the message from Will.

I hope you're having a good morning. Drive Safe.

She smiled, though the novelty of it had been ruined by his aunt.

I'm having an interesting morning. Thanks.

He was quick to respond.

Good interesting or bad interesting?

I'm not sure yet.

Elsie wasn't sure of a lot of things. She wasn't sure what to make of Will Darcy. She wasn't sure where this thing, whatever it was between them, was going. But she sure as heck wouldn't let Catherine De Bourgh decide.

She told Jane all about her breakfast with Charlotte on the way back to Meryton while Jane drove at a leisurely pace. Lydia had left them behind a few minutes into the trip, too impatient to caravan.

CHAPTER 25 ♥ PESKY HOUSE GUESTS

Charlie came back to L.A. the day after Elsie left and became an immediate fixture in Will and Gianna's home.

He liked to watch Gianna cook and throw out suggestions as if he knew better. Gianna just laughed and went on as usual.

Will had developed a pattern of calling Elsie every other evening and talking to her while she pressed and packaged T-shirts. She was working like mad to catch up on Black Friday orders, and at first, seemed too busy to talk for long. But as he got to know her better, he realized that abruptness was more likely nerves. He made her a little nervous. He hoped in a good way. So, he kept the topics pretty superficial and fun.

They never discussed the future or their feelings for one another, and on his end, it was purposeful. He would not do that over the phone. He would see her in person again, whether she believed it or not. Will had always considered the long game in all aspects of his life, and he was content to warm Elsie up by degrees.

He liked finding out new things about her, like her love of hot chocolate, or how much she hated the goofy TV morning shows Jane was addicted to watching.

One night, he discovered her secret fear of spiders, despite being a spider pacifist. She suddenly screamed as they were talking and hung up on him. He immediately called back, afraid an intruder was in the house or something.

"Elsie, are you okay?"

"Yes," she whispered, slightly out of breath. "A spider jumped onto my lap and scared me to death."

"Did you kill it?"

"Kill it? No. It jumped onto another box and I'm releasing it outside. Hold on." She came back after a minute. "Okay, I'm back. All taken care of."

"Why'd you release it? The thing probably hitched a ride inside one of those packing boxes you have sitting there, and now it's an invasive species out to wreck the local ecosystem."

"You're saying I'm the bad guy here?"

"I'm sorry. I take it back, Elsie. It was very kind of you to not immediately squish the poor thing."

"That's better."

He paused, enjoying her scolding. Charlie came into Will's room and plopped down on the end of the bed. Will glared at him and made a shooing motion.

"Who is that?" Charlie mouthed.

"Go away."

"Who needs to go away?" Elsie asked. "You better not be talking to Gianna like that."

"No, it's this pesky houseguest who won't leave."

"Oh."

The way she said it made Will realize she had assumed he meant Caroline. And he didn't want her thinking Caroline hung out in his bedroom. Earlier in the conversation, he'd mentioned he was folding laundry on his bed.

"It's Charlie. He's back from San Francisco."

"Tell Elsie I say hi," Charlie insisted.

Will rubbed his forehead. "Charlie says hi."

"Tell him, hello back. I better go, Will. The post office closes soon, and I want to get these dropped off tonight."

"Sure." Will hung up and pushed Charlie off the bed with his feet. "You are the worst friend ever."

"What did I do?" Charlie asked, picking himself up off the floor.

"You broke up with her sister. I'd rather pretend you don't exist, where Elsie's concerned."

"Well." Charlie crossed his arms. "That makes you the bad friend."

"Tell me the truth, Charlie. Have you dated anyone since Jane?"

Charlie picked up a paperweight off Will's desk and turned it over in his hands. "No."

"Why not? No nice girls up in San Francisco?"

"There are nice girls everywhere, but they're not Jane."

"So, have you done anything about that?"

Charlie set down the paperweight and picked up a framed picture of Will and Gianna as children. "A few weeks ago I broke down and texted Jane, just to say hello. She was so happy to hear from me and I freaked out, realizing what I'd done to her and ... well, I tried to put the whole thing out of my mind."

"Charlie! How could you do that?"

"I know, I know."

"You haven't contacted her since?"

Charlie shook his head. "She deserves better than me. I never should have texted her."

"Do you want to be with her or not?"

Charlie didn't answer for a long time. "If I could go back in time I'd have never broken up with Jane. I'd be making trips to Meryton every weekend, even if it meant I only got a few hours with her."

Will let out a deep breath, a weight lifting off his chest. "Then let's fix this. I'm not going to pretend it's not selfishness on my part. I'm trying to mend things with Elsie. I'm even toying with the idea of buying that stupid little rental house we stayed in. But none of that will matter if the two of you can't be in the same room together."

"Wow."

"Yeah."

Charlie rubbed his head. "So what do I do?"

Will felt like Gianna as he formulated a matchmaking plan in his head. "Don't text. Call her and have an honest conversation. Grovel. And if she still likes you, pack up and leave for Meryton."

"What about you?"

"I'm not showing up there yet. You have to go on your own. Jane will need a big gesture to believe you're serious."

A door slammed down the hall. "Will? Charlie? Are you two down here?" Caroline's voice was getting closer.

"Don't breathe a word of this to Caroline."

Charlie saluted. "Not a word."

***

Elsie hummed as she walked in the door, juggling her library books so she could pull her keys out of the lock. "Jane, you here?"

"Back here."

Elsie set down the books and headed to the kitchen. Jane was sitting at the table with a spoon and a carton of ice cream.

"Wow, what's the occasion?"

Jane looked up with forlorn eyes. "The occasion is my life. Oh, Elsie. Why now?" She pushed the carton away from her and Elsie picked it up and found the lid. The dregs weren't worth saving, so she threw it in the trash.

"What happened, Jane?"

Jane let out a sigh that seemed to go on forever. "A couple weeks ago, Charlie texted me. I answered right away. Like a fool, I said it was good to hear from him. That I missed him. And then... nothing back. It hurt so bad. I didn't want you to know."

"Jane..."

"I know, I know. But I finally felt like that was it. I could put everything past me and move on. Then today, my phone rang. When I saw his name, I didn't answer."

"Good." Elsie remembered Charlie's cheerful voice in the background when Will called yesterday. That louse.

How could two friends be so different? Will was solid. A man of his word. And Charlie was just... not.

Jane's phone rang again. "It's him. This is the third time he's tried to call. What do I do?"

Elsie wanted to tell her to ignore it, but someone needed to tell Charlie to stop calling, and based on Jane's current mood, it shouldn't be her. "Do you want me to answer?"

The phone stopped ringing.

"If he calls again, I'm handing it to you." Jane got up and rubbed her belly. "I can't believe I ate that whole carton. Let's go jogging or something tonight. I don't want to act like a depressed person anymore, even if I am."

Elsie linked arms with her sister. "Why don't we get some work done first? Twelve more T-shirt orders came in."

Jane made a face. "Maybe we should find out more from the T-shirt company that wants to buy us out."

"You want to sell our baby?" Elsie was teasing, but inside, her heart ached a little. She'd dragged Jane into this with her, knowing all along it was more her dream than Jane's. And they were in that awkward growing phase, where it was getting to be too much for the two of them, but not big enough to hire on more people.

"We could at least hear him out, Elsie."

"Tell him I want a million dollars."

"Like that's going to happen." Jane stood in front of the T-shirt press and flipped it on. "Back to work."

***

Caroline and Gianna came back from the salon with elaborate up-dos and proceeded to use the rest of the afternoon on their makeup. Will would never understand why beauty took so long.

He popped his head into the bathroom to check on them and met Gianna's gaze in the mirror. "Do you need help with the dress?"

Normally Gianna wore loose fitting clothes and had no problem dressing herself, but the glittering gown in the closet was heavy and rigid. She hadn't even tried it on until the day after she bought it, with Becky's help.

"Becky's on her way. Thanks though."

"When does Hector get here?"

Caroline finished putting in her earrings and turned to look at him. "Hector and Quinton will be here at seven."

He knew she wanted him to ask about Quinton, so he reluctantly obliged. "Is your date a mailman too?"

Caroline rolled her eyes. "No. We're talking about Quinton Verona, the tennis pro."

Will had no idea who Quinton Verona was, but he nodded anyway. "Sounds hot."

"He is," Caroline answered as she dabbed at her face with something.

The doorbell rang, and he retreated to go let in Becky. Charlie was walking up behind her, hands in his pockets.

"Hi, Becky."

She grunted in a friendly way and headed straight past Will. Charlie stood on the walkway, staring at a pot of flowers.

"You coming in or what?" Will asked.

"I don't know."

Will closed the door and came out to join him. "She hates you then?"

163

"Won't answer my calls. I sent flowers. Confirmation email says they delivered them an hour ago."

Will held his tongue. Was Charlie giving up so easily?

"What if you called Elsie and explained?" Charlie asked.

"Can't do that."

Charlie's shoulders dropped. "Yeah, maybe that would make this worse."

Will hid a smile. The Elsie he knew would encourage Jane not to answer. And either way, this was between Charlie and Jane.

"When did you last try calling her?"

"Two hours ago."

"Okay, I'd wait until tomorrow. Quit worrying about it until then. You have some tennis player to vet. He's coming to pick up your sister. I'll be questioning our delivery man."

"What?" Charlie rubbed his face. "Never mind. I don't want to know."

CHAPTER 26 ♥ GARBAGE MAN

Jane caved. It was the flowers. Instead of roses, he'd sent yellow tulips, her favorite. She cried for thirty minutes, and then spent an hour fretting about whether she should wait for him to call again. Jane ended up calling him. When Elsie went to bed at eleven, they were still talking on the phone.

She stared at the ceiling, listening to Jane laughing in the other room, and tried not to wonder why Will hadn't called. He didn't call every night. But it would have been nice to discuss Charlie and Jane. Elsie was afraid this was one of Charlie's whims. If Charlie broke Jane's heart all over again, it would be much harder for Jane to ever go back to the sweet, trusting person Elsie loved. And Will would understand that. He'd be able to tell her if she had a reason to worry.

Jane came in and woke Elsie up early the next morning. "He's coming."

"Who's coming?" Elsie asked, rolling over and covering her head with her pillow.

"Get up. I want to go grocery shopping and prepare a welcome basket for Charlie. He's renting the house down the street again."

That had Elsie sitting up. "Wow. When did you two decide that?"

Jane sat on the bed and shivered like an excited puppy. "Oh, Elsie. He talked to the homeowner before I'd even answered his calls, just in case."

"What about his job?"

"They're letting him work from home, like a satellite office. He'll still have to travel from time to time, but he says he wants to be wherever I am."

"That's... amazing." Elsie gave her a hug and couldn't help smiling at the beaming angelic happiness radiating off of Jane.

They drove to the store and bought Charlie enough groceries to fill his fridge. Then Elsie went off to work, kind of glad she'd miss the grand reunion. She didn't want to be a third wheel to that, though the alternative was mopping a restaurant floor and dealing with cranky customers. It was strange to think Will had once been one of those. A cranky customer ruining her evening.

The farther away she got from their dinner date, the harder it was to trust her instincts. Will was always friendly on the phone, but their calls didn't go into the wee hours of the morning. They didn't whisper sweet nothings or giggle and flirt. In short, Will was not Charlie. And though she wouldn't want him to be, she could never decide who was the one pulling back from the other. Maybe they were better off as friends. The thought weighed heavily on her. She didn't want to be just friends, and she definitely did not want to be just phone friends.

Will called as she was pulling into her driveway after work, apologizing for the lateness of the hour. She told him about her shift. He asked if it was raining there, as L.A. was getting drenched. She looked up at the clouds, wondering how they'd reduced themselves to conversing about the weather.

"Did Charlie make it?" Will finally asked.

"I'm not sure. I'm just walking in."

She heard giggling in the kitchen and made as much noise as possible before entering. Jane and Charlie were cutting out sugar cookies. From the looks of things, a food fight involving flour had occurred at some point.

"Oh, Elsie! Come join us." Jane leaned over and whispered something in Charlie's ear. He laughed and playfully swiped at a spot of flour across Jane's cheek. There was about to be a lot of kissing.

"Looks like fun, you two. I'm gonna shower and head to bed. I'll see you in the morning."

"Is that Will on the phone?" Charlie asked.

Elsie remembered the phone she was still holding up to her ear. "Um, yeah. Good night, Will."

"Good night." He hung up, and she dropped her phone in her purse, feeling very tired as she heard Charlie and Jane whispering about her and Will. They sounded way too hopeful about the whole thing. Why was Charlie the one here, and not Will?

***

Hector was over again. He and Gianna were decorating the house for Christmas, with Gianna directing and Hector climbing the ten-foot ladder, risking life and limb to put up whatever she wanted.

To Will's dismay and relief, he liked the guy. Hector truly cared for Gianna. He was respectful and patient. He'd even come to Caroline's rescue the night of the charity event, when her tennis player got slobberingly drunk and told Caroline exactly what he expected in exchange for his company. According to Gianna, Hector lifted him by his collar and deposited him in a cab outside.

Will should have been the one there to do it. No longer would he avoid public events. If Gianna was going, so would he. He RSVP'd for a spring benefit concert he knew Gianna would like. With any luck, he'd have Elsie as his date for it.

Waiting on Charlie was slowly killing him inside. He'd promised himself he'd give them a week, but somehow it had turned into two. There were contractors to meet with, and an unavoidable two-day trip to Phoenix. Then there was the family charity. Will had the best people overseeing the trade school, but there were still meetings and plans, decisions they left to his discretion. If he was heading to Meryton for the unforeseeable future, that meant tying up loose ends first.

Charlie rarely called with an update, but from what Elsie described, the two lovebirds were disgustingly happy together. Will wasn't sure if Elsie was suspicious or jealous. He hoped it was jealous. He knew he was.

Will wasn't a phone person. It was something Gianna had teased him about on more than one occasion. He liked to look a person in the eye, let the conversation die down and pick back up again, where looks and body language could replace the words. When there were lulls in their phone conversations, sometimes Elsie abruptly said good night and hung up. He smiled to himself. She was less of a phone person than he was. And he couldn't wait to see her again.

***

Christmas time meant the annual Bennet talent show, a party Elsie dreaded with every fiber of her being. It was her mother's brainchild. Mary was coming home to recite select pieces of her poetry. Jane dutifully agreed to sing. Lydia would be performing a scene from her favorite movie. Elsie planned to suddenly come down with the flu.

She'd participated the last two years. If anyone deserved a reprieve, she did. Especially after seeing who had RSVP'd. Charlie would be there to support Jane, of course. The Lucas clan always came, along with many of the other neighbors. But Charlotte and Collin were coming this year and participating in the show. Elsie could only imagine what Collin might do with a little undivided attention.

Charlotte would also undoubtedly grill Elsie about Will. And there was nothing to tell her. He still called. It was the highlight of her day. She loved his droll sense of humor and his insightful take on things. But she was here and he was there. Just as she'd feared, there was no future in a long distance relationship. It only led to heartache. It made her slightly more understanding of Charlie's wishy-washy treatment of Jane.

The night of the party, Elsie put on her pajamas and hid in her bed. Jane came to check on her. She looked beautiful in a bright red Christmas dress.

"You're really pulling the I'm-too-sick-to-get-up gag this year, Elsie?"

"Lock the door behind you."

Jane didn't leave. She came over and sat on the bed, pulling the covers off of Elsie's face. "Are you okay?"

"No, I'm sick."

"That's not what I meant." Jane peered into Elsie's face. "You'd tell me if there was something, right?"

Elsie nodded, swallowing hard. "I'm okay. I just really hate poetry."

Jane smiled. "I know you do." She reluctantly left. Elsie heard the lock click after the front door shut.

She waited five minutes, and then got up and headed for the kitchen. It was a shame to miss out on all that party food. Nothing in the fridge looked good. She finally settled on a Hot Pocket. Wow, this was the saddest Saturday night she could remember.

While the microwave hummed, Elsie retrieved her tablet from her room and searched for something to read.

The front door lock turned right after the microwave dinged, and Elsie's shoulders slumped. Jane must have been bullied into giving up her keys. But it was Jane who rushed in the door, not their mother.

"Elsie! You have to come now." Jane grabbed her by the arm and started pulling her toward the front door, regardless of the fact that Elsie was in pajama pants and a 'procrastinators believe in tomorrow' T-shirt

"What are you doing?"

"Will's here."

"What?"

"He's at the party. Mom's putting him in the show. Get your sorry butt over there right now."

Elsie panicked and ran down the hall, smacking her arm on the door jamb as she turned the corner too fast. She yanked a red sweater off a hanger and had it over her head before she realized she'd have to take her T-shirt off first. Will had come while she was hiding in her house microwaving a Hot Pocket.

***

This was the worst party ever, but Will set aside those immediate feelings and reminded himself not to be a snob. This wasn't about entertainment or prestige, he was here for Elsie. He realized the reason he'd been so unhappy in social situations all his life was not just his introverted nature. It was his selfish nature, the one that always graded things on an unfair scale. Nothing would ever measure up to the perfect ideal in his head.

Elsie's family was weird. But then, most families were. His sister, the best person he knew, was a recovered alcoholic. And when his parents had been alive, they'd thrown lavish parties that were ten times less interesting than this.

"Here's the guitar." Mrs. Bennet handed it over, and Will strummed it, checking the tune. She'd accosted him as soon as he walked in the door, asking if he had a talent to share. He should have known she'd find a guitar. Heck, if he'd asked for a bassoon or a French horn, she'd probably find a way to get those as well.

He hadn't played in a while and never for a crowd. He quietly strummed, trying to remember chords while keeping an eye on the door. Jane had totally lied to him when she said Elsie was running late. If Elsie had planned on coming to this party, she would have mentioned it when they talked on the phone.

"You play guitar?" Elsie's little sister wiped a smudge of chocolate off her lip and looked up at him with wide eyes. "Oh, I'm Kat, by the way. And you're the dude Lydia vandalized. Sorry about that."

Will bit back a smile. "Nice to see you again."

"What are you going to play?"

He tapped the edge of the guitar. "I only know two songs. 'Dust in the Wind' and 'Ain't No Sunshine.'"

"Ooh. Bill Withers. I love that song. Those are both kinda downer songs for a party, though."

"You know who Bill Withers is?"

Kat shrugged. "Music's my thing. Not playing or singing. I'm totally tone deaf. But I can name any singer or song from any era. It's a gift."

"So 'Dust in the Wind' is by…"

"Kansas, duh."

"Okay, name three other songs by Kansas."

She raised an eyebrow. "'Carry On My Wayward Son,' 'Point of No Return,' and 'Song For America.'"

Will was officially impressed. "I only know the first one. I'll take your word on the other two."

Charlie tapped him on the shoulder. "She's here."

Will looked toward the door and caught Elsie staring at him. She looked beautiful in her red sweater and fitted jeans. He smiled and gave a little wave.

"What's your talent for tonight then?" he asked, turning back to Kat.

"My talent is being a part of the audience and clapping loud. All I have to do is threaten to sing and I'm off the hook. Oh, and I'd go with 'Ain't No Sunshine.' The girls will melt."

She blended back into the crowd, and Will tried to make his way over to Elsie. It was a little hard with the guitar. He held it straight up and down so the neck wouldn't hit anyone. The house wasn't big enough for the number of people they'd crammed inside, especially with the makeshift stage taking up a quarter of it.

Mr. Bennet stood a few feet ahead of him, smiling, but beneath his smile was a look of pain Will recognized. When Gianna pushed herself too hard she often had the same look.

All the chairs in the room were occupied. Will came over and put a light hand on Mr. Bennet's shoulder. "Man, it's crowded in here."

"Yes, it is. My wife lives for this." His eyes widened when he realized who he was talking to. "Will, I'm so sorry about your car."

"Don't worry about it. Though I did want to talk to you about something. Can we head over here?"

Mr. Bennet nodded and followed as Will made a path over to where a set of kitchen chairs lined the wall, all occupied. Collin and Charlotte were sitting with their heads together, looking over a paper on Charlotte's lap, but Will's eyes gravitated to their feet. They were both wearing tap shoes.

"Hi, Charlotte."

She looked up and smiled. "Nice to see you again, Will."

Collin stuck out a hand, and Will shook it. "Your Aunt Catherine has been trying to get ahold of you. She's mentioned her frustration to me several times."

Will nodded. "Thanks for letting me know." He looked to Charlotte again and motioned with his head to Mr. Bennet.

"Oh, Collin. We should get something to drink before the show starts."

"Yes, of course, my lovey. We do need to stay hydrated." He stood up and she followed.

Will gave her a smile of thanks and watched as Mr. Bennet slowly lowered himself into a chair with a groan. "So, Will. What did you want to talk to me about?"

Oh. Will hadn't thought that far ahead. "Well, I … Citrus, actually. I have this lemon tree in my backyard, and I was going to ask you about fertilizer."

***

Every time Elsie found him in the crowd, Will was talking to someone else. This time Mr. and Mrs. Lucas. Jane had made it sound like he'd come for her. But maybe he was just visiting Charlie again. It served her right. She'd pushed him away enough times that it was only fair she ended up here. Disappointed. Regretful. Heartsick. A man could only be so patient. Their opportunity had passed and all he had to offer her was friendship. She should have attacked him by her car instead of slinking into her seat and not kissing him goodnight. Regrets were the worst.

Seeing him up close again was killing her inside. He looked so handsome. So at ease with her family. Which was majorly weird.

Kat passed by, and Elsie held onto her arm. "What were you and Will talking about?"

"Oh, just music stuff. He's nice."

"Yeah, nice."

She looked over to find him again, but he was getting lined up with the other talent show performers. Her least favorite part of the night was about to begin.

Her mom blew into the microphone, causing everyone to put their hands over their ears. "Can everyone hear me?" She smiled in satisfaction and welcomed everyone. Then with a grand gesture of her arm, she turned the show over to Charlotte and Collin.

Charlotte had been in dance lessons all through childhood. She and Elsie took tap and ballet together, though Elsie gave it up around age six. So it was no surprise to see Charlotte tap in a circle around Collin while he marched in place, looking way too pleased with himself. He spotted her and winked. Creep.

Mary was next, reciting her poem, "Loud and Alone." And it was loud, every punctuated word making the speaker pop. Elsie cringed, wishing she could walk up there and pull the microphone back from Mary a couple inches, or maybe a couple feet. She caught Will's eye, and he pressed his lips together as if he was trying not to laugh. He pointed to his guitar, and she raised an eyebrow. Then he pointed to her, and then the stage.

"No way," she mouthed.

"Come on," he mouthed back.

She couldn't help blushing a little as she shook her head. When would this party end so she could finally talk to him?

Jane and Charlie sang a bad karaoke duet of "I've Got You Babe," and then Lydia, in a silk jumpsuit that likely cost more than Elsie's entire wardrobe, strutted on stage to perform lines from *Too Brave to Back Down*, the true story of a backup dancer who became a star. Or something like that. Elsie had only made it about ten minutes into the movie, though Lydia could quote it word for word.

Lydia sobbed into the microphone, blubbering something about how no one would hold her back from her dream or her dream man. The crying was actually pretty good, the result of years of practicing it on her parents when she wanted something.

Will stared at the floor. It was the first time Elsie had caught him looking uncomfortable tonight. And she couldn't blame him one bit. Lydia finally finished, and Elsie clapped, so happy it was almost over. Will would be closing the show.

He walked on stage and pulled out a folding chair, adjusting the microphone to his sitting height. He looked down at the guitar as he started, strumming the first few notes of a familiar song. The crowd instantly quieted. When he began to sing, his eyes landed on Elsie and stayed there.

She froze, her insides turning to mush as he gave her a look that could only be described as a smolder.

***

Every note, every word was for her. Will tuned out everyone else, even Mrs. Bennet's loud voice commenting on how well Lydia did.

He strummed the last note and a couple of teenage girls in the front screamed and reached out their hands to him. He gave them a reluctant wave and stood up, handing the guitar back to an eager Mrs. Bennet. She thanked everyone for coming and held onto him, preventing him from leaving the stage. After she put the microphone back in its stand, she smiled up at him. "Would you mind taking the trash out, Will? The one in the kitchen is overflowing."

CHAPTER 27 ♥ PLASTIC CHAIRS

"Have you seen Will?" Elsie glanced around again, but she still couldn't find him. There'd been so many well-wishers congratulating him on his performance, and then he'd disappeared.

Lydia rolled her eyes. "Nope. I can't believe he upstaged me like that. I told Mom I wanted to go last. You're supposed to leave the best for last."

Okay, asking Lydia had been a mistake, but Charlie and Jane didn't know where he was, and all Kat knew was that she'd last seen Will headed toward the kitchen.

"I really hoped I'd never have to see that guy again. It's bad enough I have to be indebted to him forever."

"Indebted to him?" Elsie stopped peering around and stared at Lydia.

Lydia froze, putting a hand to her lips. "It's nothing." But her face said differently.

Elsie stared her down and Lydia squirmed, avoiding her gaze.

"I could have another talk with Mom and Dad about your spending habits."

"Okay, fine. Whatever. Will's the one who paid for my bail, and the fees, and the lawyer and all that. Happy now?"

Happy? Elsie's knees started to buckle, and she reached out and put a hand on Lydia's shoulder. "Why would he do that?"

"I don't know. Let go. You're going to wrinkle my outfit."

Elsie let go and Lydia stalked off. Elsie did another scan of the room. Her mom waved her over and Elsie reluctantly went to see what she wanted.

"Jane said you're looking for Will, dear. I asked him to take the garbage out."

Elsie's mouth dropped open. "What?"

"Don't look at me like that. He's a strong young man. He didn't mind."

Elsie ran outside and around to the side where they kept the garbage can. Will was just shutting the lid. He turned around and stopped short when he saw her standing there.

"I liked your song."

"Thanks."

He walked forward until they were standing together, his eyes never leaving hers. Her heartbeat sped up and she twisted her hands together in front of her, suddenly nervous.

"I'm sorry my mom put you on garbage duty."

"Someone had to do it." He shrugged. "And look, now we can talk to each other."

"We could have talked inside." She wanted to kick herself. Why was she scolding him?

Will gave a hint of a smile. "I was trying to be sociable, but it's like studying a language. It takes all my concentration, and afterward, I feel drained."

"I feel the same way."

"I did want to talk to you. I still do. Can we go for a walk?"

"Yes."

Their hands brushed, and he took hers, leading her toward the gate. "Do you mind holding hands with someone who just took out the trash?"

She laughed. "I'll brave the germs."

He reached up and undid the latch, and they walked through to the front yard.

"Elsie, I want you to be honest with me. Sometimes you give mixed signals, and if you'd rather be friends, or not even that, I'll understand."

"Mixed signals?"

"My feelings have not changed since throwing myself at you in the library. But I don't know how you feel about me."

"I feel…" They'd been calling each other for weeks with no indication of what it meant, to either of them. She wanted more than friendship. She wanted a love stronger than even the giddy happiness Jane and Charlie shared. Was it possible with Will? She needed to be brave. She needed to just say it.

Laughter drifted over from her house, and they continued walking down the street where they could be alone. Her parent's neighbors were way too enthusiastic about Christmas. Tinkly music accompanied their light display, and Winnie the Pooh in a Santa hat wobbled back and forth from the porch.

His hold on her hand loosened and she gripped it tighter before he could pull away completely. "Thank you for what you did for Lydia," she blurted out.

"I wanted to put it behind us. Jeff influences people to do things they normally wouldn't."

"You give Lydia too much credit." Elsie sighed. "And yourself not enough."

He shook his head. "I was an idiot when I first met you. I've been trying to make up for it ever since."

"Will, if we turn this into an apology contest, I'm pretty sure I'd win." They were almost to her house, and she tugged him onto the lawn. "I have chairs in the back. Let's go sit on my porch."

The butterflies gathering in her stomach went into a full-on flurry when they reached the dark backyard. Will stopped and pulled her closer. The smell of his cologne filled her senses, and he leaned down, his lips inches from hers.

"So, what is this, Elsie? Friendship?"

She shook her head. "I want more. I want to be wherever you are. I hate the phone."

His careful gaze broken into a hopeful smile. "You can't kiss a phone."

She closed the distance between them, pressing her lips to his. He took over, kissing her in a way that told her exactly how much he'd missed her. He told her lots of things, and she told them right back, until the heat made her feel like she was about to combust. He pulled away and smiled.

She gripped his shirt and reached up on her tiptoes, demanding an encore.

"Elsie," he whispered against her lips. "I love you. I know it's too soon to say it."

"Not too soon," she murmured. He kissed her jawline, and she sighed. "I love you, too. I think it happened when you took me on in basketball. I was so mad at Caroline for showing up."

His laughter tickled her neck. "You didn't show it when we said goodnight. That's why I've been so careful on the phone."

She leaned back to get a good look at his face, trying to understand what he meant. "Careful, as in, super platonic?"

"It wasn't just me, you know, Miss I-have-work-to-do-Bye."

She bit her lip. "Yeah, well, I saw what happened to Jane. I didn't want my heart stomped on like that. I thought I was protecting us both."

"Charlie is a lucky dog. She should have never taken him back."

"But you encouraged him to try, didn't you?"

He looked like he wanted to deny it, but he finally nodded. "Yeah."

Together they walked to the plastic chairs on the back porch and the motion lights kicked on. Elsie dusted hers off, feeling slightly embarrassed. Their backyard was nothing to get excited about. The lawn was covered in weeds she'd been too busy to pull out or spray. "Your aunt thinks I'm not good enough for you."

"Oh, is that what she's been trying to pester me about? I stopped taking her calls a long time ago. She kept telling Gianna if she only worked harder, she'd get out of that wheelchair." He scooted his plastic chair closer and took her hand, keeping her palm open and running his fingers along it. "Don't worry about my aunt. Though it's good to know she still cares so much about my love life."

"Seriously, Will. I know you hate this town. I'll always have to be somewhat close to my parents, cleaning up after Lydia's messes and making sure my dad's okay."

"You take care of so many people, Elsie. Who takes care of you?" He slowly kissed the inside of her palm and every nerve in her body stood at attention. How had she gotten so lucky?

"Will Darcy, you are… you are a perfect man."

He laughed. "Far from it. But you should say it again. Come over here." He patted his lap, and she changed seats, wrapping her arms around his neck. "I bought that ugly house," he whispered.

"What house?"

"The rental. That way Charlie and I can come and go as we please."

She stared into his face to make sure he was serious. "But you didn't know how I felt about you."

He kissed her softly. "I'm a hopeful guy."

And then the stupid plastic chair collapsed. Elsie screamed as they went down together, hitting the cement.

"Ohh." Will groaned, reaching back to rub his tailbone. He'd broken her fall. "That's gonna leave a big bruise."

"Are you okay?"

He winced. "Yeah, I think so. But let's get you some new patio furniture."

She laughed and carefully helped him back up.

"Elsie! Elsie Bennet, are you hiding back here with Will Darcy? Everyone is looking for you two." Her mom came around the corner, hands on her hips. She spied the broken lawn chair. "I don't wanna know what you two are up to. But the party's over, and I could use some help cleaning up."

Will winked at Elsie. "Yes, ma'am."

EPILOGUE ♥

Elsie demonstrated how to use the T-shirt press and then moved aside so her students could try it out. Teaching had never been something she'd considered, especially teaching adults. But she also never thought she'd be marrying Will Darcy in a few short weeks. She couldn't help holding up her left hand and watching the diamonds sparkle as they caught the light.

Will didn't tell her about his trade school or his other charity work until they'd dated for several months. He was quite the mystery man, and every day, the love he showed her was the greatest mystery of all. She'd gladly spend the rest of her life trying to match it.

"Miss Bennet, I think the font needs to be bigger." One of her students held up his shirt, and she studied it.

"I think you're right. But put it on to check."

"Really?"

"Yeah, just throw it on over the shirt you're wearing. It's the best way to know if the size of the design is working."

When she and Jane sold the T-shirt business for an outrageous amount of money, Elsie had to give up the rights to her T-shirt designs as well. At first it had felt like giving away all her hopes and dreams, but she found creating for herself, without the pressure of a deadline was freeing. More importantly, Jane, with a nice little nest egg, could go back to teaching kindergarten, something she'd truly missed. The elementary school was over-the-moon to have her.

It was Gianna's idea to have Elsie teach graphic design and small business start-up at the trade school. Now, making T-shirts was strictly for fun. She and the students took their favorite new designs and created merchandise to sell at fundraisers for the school.

One of her students touched her arm. "Um, you have a visitor, Miss Bennet."

Elsie turned around and caught Will watching her from the doorway. His smile had her tongue tied all in knots, and she blushed red as knowing glances came from all around the room. Class ended in two minutes. Without being told, her students immediately began shutting down the computers and gathering their bags.

"Enjoy your weekend, dear." An older lady patted her on the back.

Oh, she planned to. She and Will were driving to Meryton together, and though that meant checking in on her family to see what mischief Lydia was into now, and packing up the last of her stuff, anything was better with Will by her side.

She pulled her purse out of the bottom drawer of her desk, and Will came inside, shutting the door behind him.

"Will," she warned.

He grinned and came closer.

"Do you know how many times we've been caught making out in this building?"

He took her hands and wrapped them around his waist. "Not often enough if you ask me." He kissed her thoroughly, and she suddenly couldn't remember why she'd ever not wanted him to. Witnesses? What were those?

"Can't we elope?" she whispered as he kissed just below her bottom lip and then in the soft hollow of her neck. They'd agreed to wait until after they were married to take things further, but the waiting was killing them both.

"No. Because I love you, and in twenty years you'd look back and regret it." He reluctantly pulled away, keeping her hand as they walked out to his car.

"I don't think I'd regret it."

"You'll want your family there. And the flowers. And your beautiful dress I'm not allowed to see."

She sighed. "I know. But a girl can dream. So, do you think Charlie will propose to Jane soon?"

He opened the passenger door for her and then went around and got in. "Oh, I know he will. He's just waiting until after our wedding."

"Poor Kat. She's enjoyed living with Jane. I didn't think it would work out, but she's such a better person when she's not hanging around Lydia so much."

"Has she considered college?"

"Last time I talked to her, she wanted to be a physical therapist. But before that, it was veterinary school, beauty school, and law school."

"She'll figure it out."

Elsie smiled at him, amazed at the support he gave her family, whether they deserved it or not. He'd told her on more than one occasion that Kat was a misunderstood genius. He patiently allowed her mom to treat him like a servant, tolerated Lydia, and listened when Mary talked his ear off about weird subjects, but he genuinely enjoyed spending time with her dad, Jane, and Kat. She couldn't ask for more than that.

He pulled up to the house, and they got out to pack a few things for the weekend. "I'll grab snacks," he said, heading for the kitchen.

Elsie went down the hall to get the suitcase she'd left on the bedroom floor where she was staying, but froze in the doorway, staring at her bed. Her pillowcase had been switched out with a new one. Will's handsome, insanely angry face glared back at her, above the words, "The Me Monster."

"Will!"

He came up behind her, leaning down to rest his chin on her shoulder. "It would be a shame to let such a beautiful piece of art stay hidden on your computer."

"It's terrible."

"It reminds me of how we met."

"Does this mean I get to dig my old 'Me Monster' T-shirt out of my drawer and wear it home?"

His laughter tickled her ear. "I'd prefer you didn't."

"Don't worry. I've never been tempted to wear it again. I've almost thrown it out several times."

"What held you back?" he asked.

She smiled and turned to look at him. "Like you said, it reminds me of how we met."

"See?" He loved it when she admitted he was right about something.

"Thanks for the pillow. I think."

"Every marriage needs a few inside jokes, Els." He leaned down to kiss her, and as he did, he picked her up, carrying her back to the front door.

"My suitcase," she protested.

"I'll get it. Grab the snacks, temptress."

She laughed and headed to the kitchen to retrieve the cooler from the island counter. Her imagination was already working on ways to surprise him back. Life as Mrs. Darcy would be quite the adventure.

Thank you, readers. I love Pride and Prejudice and creating my own version of Jane Austen's characters was a blast. Reviews are much appreciated. If you'd like to hear about new releases, you can follow my Amazon author page:
www.amazon.com/author/racheljohn

Other titles by Rachel John:

Sworn to Loathe You:
Worst Neighbor Ever (A Prequel)
I Hated You First
Carpool Crush
Not Friends
Keep It Together
Freelance Flirt

Austen Inspired Romantic Comedies:
Emma the Matchmaker
Persuading the Captain
Dashing into Disaster

A Change in Plans:
An Unlikely Alliance
Her Charming Distraction
Protector of Her Heart
Pretending He's Mine

Reality TV Romances:
Bethany's New Reality
Matchmaker for Hire
Gorgeous and the Geek

Christmas Matched by Mistake:
The Stand-in Christmas Date
The Christmas Bachelor Auction
The Christmas Wedding Planners
The Accidental Christmas Match Up
The Backup Christmas Crush

Made in the USA
Monee, IL
07 February 2025

11751231R00105